THIS 'ISH IS PERSONAL

By Prisca James

<u>This 'Ish Is Personal</u>
Written by
Prisca James

Preface

Alexis Nolan is a mother of three with beauty, brains, and sense of class few people in her circle possessed. She, as a wife, spent her whole adult life devoted to her family until meeting Candace McHenry and Keisha Stokes. Who she believed were her friends until an unsuspected secret was revealed about her. Causing Alexis to do things that aided in the demise of her elite image sending the friendships between the women into a downward spiral.

This contemporary novel is full of secrets, lies and promiscuity. It supplies a great reading experience for all making "This 'Ish Is Personal" a sweeping story about these women of diverse backgrounds and their struggles with men, lies, love, money, and sex a must read.

CHAPTER 1

Candace McHenry

"Why is it always me?" I said in my Terry McMillan voice as I walked in. "Damn." The Central Bookings and the doors closed behind me. I sat on the ice-cold bench tucking my new sweatsuit pants under my toes as I observed the bench making certain not to lock eyes with none of the bitches in the cell. I began wishing that the ugly correction officer, who clearly didn't like me had let me keep my new sweatshirt I had on since it was brick cold in here. The air was thin and very chilly. After taking my seat, I noticed the woman next to me had feces all over her. Which would explain why this was the only vacancy in the whole cell.

Another night on the town with my girls ended up in a trip down to the Central Bookings. I told myself the last time I was out that I was not getting into another of this bitch's beefs. But here I am! Just as I finished that last thought, I heard the clashing of the cell door open and in came her fat ***. Yeah, Keisha. She plopped her big tail right next to me on the bench, causing everyone to move down. The sight of her made my whole attitude change from a calm but upset demeanor into a rage. Since she was the reason, I was sitting here in the first place. I thought to myself. I'm about to open a can of Whoop Ass on this girl. But, quickly decided against it since it was the reason, I was sitting in this cell in the first place.

See, Keisha was the type of person that befriended everyone; however, she was the worst type of friend to have. She was a leech. She was always coming off to everyone as a warm, compassionate, friendly person. But she was the complete opposite, which you might call a wolf in sheep's clothing. This Bitch took it to the next level. Keisha always knows how to say the right thing or even do the right things to get a person to do what she wants. We all called her the master of deception. This was because she could almost at an instant turn into someone else. Nothing was too great for her to be able to get anything! With the body to kill and the ass to back it up she definitely had the tools to make any man drop to his knees and she had no problem using it to do so. Girl, I already called Tyrone.! He was talking to our lawyer right now to get this taken care of. I should be out of here in an hour.

"So, what you gonna do? Who's coming to pick you up? Did you even make a phone call yet?" Keisha never seemed to amaze me. She's always looking out for herself, but never gives a damn about the little people she takes down in the process.

"Keisha, who the hell am I supposed to call? Nico? My phone was in my pocketbook that the police now have. His work number is in my phone, that the police now have. My house phone was forwarded to my cell phone that was in my bag that the police now have! Which I might add, is my very new, very expensive, Louis Vuitton purse that Nico just bought me. The point I'm trying to make is the police have all my shit bitch."

I could see the female CO's looking at my bag when we walked in placing it into my property. "Shit Candace, I'm just asking you. You always get like this when you get upset, all jumpy and stuff. You should really get that shit checked out by a doctor or something. I don't think it's normal. You might need one of them. You know what pills they'd be giving people? The ones that calm their asses down."

"Keisha, you're the only person I know who gets locked up and makes herself at home like we on some damn retreat or something. This is jail, Bitch! And yes, I'm jumpy. I don't belong here. This **** is not for me. And I'm pissed off ***. I have children, and I don't belong in nobody's jail cell."

"Candy. I know what you got. And furthermore, you didn't have to help me fight that girl. I could have handled that all on my own. So, what put you in here? Don't sit there and act like it's my fault that you are in jail. You put your damn self in here."

"Oh, OK.! So, I guess that girl size 7 Prada boot just mistakenly landed on your forehead, and her foot just slipped, going all up and through your ass?"

"Whatever. You can talk that **** to someone that wasn't there. I saw the 220 pounds ***** whoop your *** and if I wasn't there, you would be in the OR instead of down here."

By this time, my blood is boiling. I hated for someone to downsize something I had done for them. So ungrateful. "You only got like one punch in before the bouncer pulled us out of the club anyways."

I had already learned a long time ago not to argue with idiots. So, I opted to end the conversation there, but not before letting Keisha know with the most seriousness. "If I have to spend a minute past the time you get out of here, the next fight you will be having. Will be for your life. In a hospital bed."

I was so serious and meant every word of it. I was tired of her disrespect for me and my time, and the way she was acting. As if I wasn't the victim was really getting under my skin? Keisha always had the biggest mouth and the smallest bite. See, she thought she was more than what she was, and it always created problems. As I ended the conversation, while walking away to relocate to the bench across the room, I could feel Keisha's eyes beaming down my back. I was aware that she knew that I wasn't playing any games with her since she had tested me before like this, which resulted in her getting 18 stitches and losing 30% of her hearing in her right ear. Yeah, she got my draft, since her next move was to go to the bars and ask the CO if she could get another phone call.

See! Despite how much we fought and argued, Keisha Stokes was one of my very close friends. I mean that I loved her like a sister. OK, maybe half-sister. But we were definitely different, and we didn't like each other at all times. But one thing was for sure, we had each other's back. I could depend on her, and she could depend on me. We met at a mutual friend's house around the neighborhood where we both were living at the time. It had to be at least twelve years ago. You could really say I met Keisha by accident. Since the first time I saw her, it was because I had to use the bathroom at my home girl's house. She was in there giving some guy head. I had been knocking on the door, more like banging on the door for close to five minutes and I was upset. Shoot I have to pee! Not believing that a person could be doing the number two for a whole hour and half. I couldn't wait any longer. Whoever was in there had to get out of that bathroom. With Mad Dog 2020 going through my system, I just couldn't hold it. I began to knock and knock and knock on the door. I was not willing to piss on myself. To my surprise, just as I had determined that I was going to kick the door down when the door flew open. There she was sitting on the edge of the tub with Donald Davis. **** in her mouth asking me, "Was there a problem?"

I told her "YES. There was a problem. I had to piss."

"My bad. Girl. That's all you had to say?" Keisha didn't even care about the five or so onlookers that had managed to congregate in front of the door. She just proceeded to pull his now limp penis out of her mouth. She got up from where she was sitting with a smirk on her face, as she passed by me. In the doorway, she simply said, "I know the feeling that 2020 must be getting to you too huh?"

All I could do was place a fake smile on my face and say yeah. When I finally got in the bathroom and sat on the toilet, all I could say to myself was that "Was that nasty hoe I've been hearing about. But damn! From what I could see. Donald sure was blessed."

After sitting there for what seemed like an eternity the endless alcohol seemed to be coming out of my system slowly, but surely. I was really getting more and more drunk. As I opened the door to come out of the bathroom, I saw her standing in the hallway looking as if she was looking for someone. I just glanced at her and began walking away when she ran up to me. "Hey, girl, Hey, girl. Candace, right?"

Surprised at the fact that she knew my name, I hesitated and said, "Yeah, Candace."

"Well, I'm Keisha. I hope you don't get the wrong idea about me. I just get a little horny when I drink. Plus, I can't lie, that man is so fine."

Keisha was right about that. He danced and sure was sexy, but whatever. "Look, Keisha, I'm not trying to be smart but that's your business. I don't have anything to do with that."

"I just wanted to tell you and also make sure that you would keep what you saw to yourself being as though my boyfriend Tyrone was out front."

I thought to myself that she must have really been drunk to not notice that I wasn't the only one who saw her. But to answer her question, I had to let her know that I didn't put my mouth in other people's business, but I did suggest to her that it would be wise to watch how she opens bathroom doors next time. Because she was lucky it was me and not Tyrone.

Keisha Stokes. Keisha Stokes. Your release. Coming back from reminiscing of the past, I heard Keisha's name called out. By the visibly no-nonsense officer. I looked up and could see Kay walking over to the gate to leave the cell. As she moved near, she began mouthing to me the words "I'm sorry."

With utter disgust, I turned my head and instantly felt my stomach begin turning. I began to feel the patron and all those obey wings from the night starting to surface in my throat. I was just about to decorate the floor when I heard the CO reopen the cell doors and yell out. Candace McHenry, you're free to go. Before he even finished my full name, I jetted to my feet and with what felt like one step, exited the cell. After leaving the cell, the correctional officer led me down a narrow, dark hallway to a small metal window with bars in front of it. Once I approached the window, I could see a man behind the desk with a badge that read Officer Lewis. I thought to myself, Officer Lewis seems very familiar to me.

I remembered his face from hanging around with the guys I grew up with at the little corner store located at the end of our block. Plus, his face was kind of hard to forget since he had the biggest dimples not to mention that as a man, he was fine as hell. He was the same one who had gone undercover and got all of them arrested and put in jail for like ten or more years. I think my one homeboy just got home. I guess after he was subpoenaed, he had to testify against all of them as a witness to them serving a undercover officer. There were talks in the neighborhood that he was found dead but, I guess that was a lie. Sensing me, glaring at him, Officer Lewis began to pay closer attention to me. I was really uncomfortable with him staring at me. So, I just decided not to make eye contact with him. I was sure that once Officer Lewis saw my face. He took a really good look at me. He would surely recognize me, and that would lead to another set of problems that I just didn't need right now.

"Name?"

With a tremor in my voice I answered, "Candace McHenry."

I could feel him looking down at me from his platform window. "Here, here's your property. One cosmetic bag, one hairbrush, one pack of birth control pills, one box of condoms and one black purse."

"A black purse! No, Sir. There's a mistake! I had a patented leather turquoise blue. Louis Vuitton purse. *** ****. I just got that purse. It was a gift." Oh Lord, this man it's gonna kill me.

Looking up at the cheap non leather purse, the officer was trying to give me, I knew exactly what happened. Those crooked *** female officers, I knew they was gonna pull one on me. "Well, this is what we have for your property, and I need you to sign for it. You may File a claim at a later date for any missing property. Would you like the paperwork?"

Floored by the whole ordeal, I asked the officer for my missing wallet as well. And his response was the same, except this time he seemed visibly disturbed by my questions. Too angry to even argue with him, I grabbed the pen and simply marked an X. On the signature line. Plus. I didn't want to bring any more attention to myself. Since Officer Lewis would surely make my life a living hell. Snatching my belongings and what wasn't mine from the table, I turned around to leave. At the end of the grayish colored hallway stood a man with a blank stare. He had absolutely no expression, making what felt like an eternity walk up to him complete disaster, just uncomfortable. While approaching him, I began putting on my jacket and my coach tennis shoes. They were minus shoelaces since the CO had made me take them out during booking, which I completely didn't blame them. Since, I know now that if I had to stay in there I would have definitely tried to use them to help end my misery. If I had to spend another minute in that cell, Lord only knows what I would have done. Now standing up before the officer with the blank stare. I was asked once more my name before exiting the doors to the jail. I had a boat load of energy when pronouncing every syllable in my name. "Candace McHenry!"

With that, the officer checked my name off his list, and I was out the doors. Thank you, Jesus! I said out loud while the door slammed behind me. Then the reality set in that I was standing downtown Baltimore with no money, no phone, no ride. What was I going to do?

It wasn't a complete surprise to me that Keisha didn't wait for me.

But damn, I did have $150 in my purse but that was gone too with my wallet. But **** that was the least of my worries now. Since all I could think of was getting home and into my bed. Just as I turned the corner to get a hack (Illegal cab), and since I had no money, I would just have him drop me down the street from my house and run off. **** who was he going to call? The police? Just as I began to approach a car that had stopped, I could hear a horn honking. I turned around just in time to see Alexis Nolan and her new BMW 760 7 series. She seemed like an Angel sent by God to me at that time, just as I needed her. I was so happy to see her. I hopped into the car and gave Alexis the biggest hug. I told her how excited I was to see her now. Inside of Alexis car I was surrounded by the new car smell and the softest premium leather I had ever felt. I had to admit to her that her car was nice, real nice. But being the type of person I am, I didn't give any compliments. I found them to just be a way to tell someone else that they were better than you and that wasn't me. Wasn't nobody better than me! So, I just kept my love for her vehicle to myself. Alexis pulled off fast, jumping over to 83 westbound, which was just fine with me since I wanted the quickest route to my house for a few miles. Things were absolutely quiet. Listening to the quiet storm and relaxing, I closed my eyes. I was not inclined to speak because I was fully aware of Lexus dislike towards Keisha, and I just wasn't in the right mindset to hear I told you so. After a few minutes of silence, Alexis blurted out. "So, you good?"

Not able to hold in my frustration anymore, I replied, "I'm done with Keisha!"

"Girl bye. No, you not, Candy and we both know 're not. Why do you keep messing with that girl? I will never know. But the one thing I do know is she means, you know, good. I don't know how many times I have to tell you that."

I wasn't surprised by Alexis's words since I had heard them almost every day since Keisha and Alexis had met.

"So, what happened anyway?"

"It doesn't matter. I'm good!"

"What's wrong with you? Why all the attitudes?"

"I just don't feel like talking, hearing you scolding me like I'm some damn school child." I could feel the anger building up within me, so I decided to withstand speaking for the rest of the ride. I was just going to listen rather than take my frustration out on Lexus. After all, she was my very best friend, going back on my word. There was one question I was curious to know the answer to, and that was how did Alexis know I was down here? But with further thought and listening to some of the things she was saying, I came to my own conclusion. When Candace got that call, she called Keisha. It wasn't hard to figure out that Keisha had called her. Because Alexis was my best friend, I didn't have to ask why she came. I already knew why, and even still I was grateful to her. But I was not going to let anyone belittle me. Not even her. I could call Alexis for anything and know that she will always be there for me and I for her. I always accepted her for who she was born with, I guess some type of defect in her leg. I felt the need to be very protective of Alexis. She walked with a limp, but it never mattered to me. Lexus was beautiful, with the most unique, prettiest big eyes. They were green and seemed to intrigue a lot of people. They were a great shape and some long Indian like hair. Her skin was the right shade of caramel brown, making her a constant threat to most women her beauty was unique ah, but compelling at the same time. Having a Spanish mother and an Italian father she had it going on. If I said it myself, I wasn't mad at her. But what was most captivating about her was that she never let it go to her head. She was amazingly humble and was a great woman of great value. I could a l w a y s count on her to give me great advice and guide me in the right direction. Not to mention, Alexis had made a great home life for herself, a husband that was a general in the army, two little boys and the most supportive close-knit family I had ever seen. I wasn't used to it. I had never seen anything like that before. She never left any stone uncovered, and I admired her for that. But Lexus and I were two complete opposites. I always believed she was the ideal friend to have, but I couldn't help but wonder, was everything really so perfect in her world, or was it all a front?

I mean, everybody held skeletons in their closet, so why not her? We pulled up in front of my house quicker than I thought, but not a minute too soon since I was at my wits end with the whole evening, even with Alexis. They say no good deed goes unpunished and this very thing I was about to set true. So, not even saying goodbye or thank you for that matter, I exited the car and slammed the door. I made a beeline into my house.

Dear diary.

If I ever come across as heartless or ungrateful. Please forgive me. I am one of God's children. So, I am guilty of sin, and the ways of my flesh should not be held against me. So, with that said, I'm so jealous of that stuck up ***** Alexis. Why is she so entitled to that life and not me?

Chapter 2

Keisha Lorraine Stokes

"What the FUCK Tyrone? What the hell took you so long? Man."

"Bitch If you don't calm your ass down! Aren't I here? You are a ungrateful, Heffer. You're lucky I'm here anyway. I should have left your *** in there.! Since we asking questions, let me ask you this. Why you keep getting locked up, huh? Cat got your tongue?"

Silence.

"This is what I thought. You can't say anything! Look at your face, Keisha! Do you really think I want a female who looks like she lost a fight with Layla Ali on my arms?"

"No, Tyrone!!! But do you think that I want a disrespectful man on mines?"

"Girl, do you think I care? If you're not happy with me, leave. I'm not sweating you!"

Yeah, Tyrone was my man and he loved me. He just had a bad way of showing it, but he loved me. We've been together for a little over two years and to be honest, I've been through hell and back with him. But there is just something about this man I can't shake him. I mean standing at 6 feet two inches tall, about 260 pounds, black skin with the perfect chin strap shape up on his face, he kept himself up. He always kept the neat, well cut, looking like he just stepped out of the barbershop every day, all day. I had to fight females off left and right since my baby was the heartthrob. But to me it was all worth it since I was myself not a looker. In my eyes at least, some may have even called me ugly. But I would say I had unique features abstractly placed on my face. Yeah, you know, like that dark skin ball headed supermodel chick. I mean, people thought she was beautiful, that dark complexion with small beady eyes, big lips, about 190 pounds and five foot six. I embrace my ugliness. I saw all of what people found a flaw, as an asset. I made the best of what I had been given. **** my big lips were good for wrapping around my man or any man I felt like member. And well, my big booty, all the dudes I dealt with found it to be a great thing. So, with a big booty, nice big lips, and a knowledge of what to do with both of them, who needs looks? I dropped out of school in the 8th grade since I had gotten pregnant by a 25-year-old guy that was friends with my cousin. Come to find out she was sleeping with him too. So, so what? I wasn't that book smart, but there was one thing that I was and that was street smart.

Growing up down South Baltimore having Street smarts was much more necessary. Opposed to knowing U.S. History or Algebra not to mention that I am a mother of six and I'm not with any of their fathers yet knowing how to make money. I started at a very young age and was always my only focus. Tyrone, Tyrone! "Where are we going?" Screaming over the New Lil Wayne CD that was playing in his truck. Tyrone!

"What man?" Finally answering me.

"Where are we going?"

"Tony's house to pick up Jewels!"

"What?"

"Girl, you heard me."

Trying to wrap my head around what He was saying was puzzling me so much to where I just had to ask the question. "Why do you have to pick up your two-year-old daughter at 4:00 in the morning?"

After pausing for what felt like an eternity, he finally responded. "Man you can go home, I'm stopping. You can get right on the bus. It doesn't make me no difference as a matter of fact, get out!"

Looking out the window, I could see the bus he was referring to passed by the passenger side window. I couldn't believe this man was trying to put me out the car. But I already knew I wouldn't be going anywhere, because him going to his baby mother's house without me wasn't an option at 4:00 in the morning. Yeah, I'm going. So the only way I will be going anywhere would be kicking and screaming. I was already prepared for a fight since Tyrone and I tend to get physical when we had disagreements, I just was trying to prepare myself mentally for the challenge, not even realizing that I was gazing at Tyrone with the look of disgust. I suddenly felt the truck come to a halt and without warning he turned around to me and slapped the SHIT out of my face. Tyrone hated to be challenged. Clenching onto my face, I was so angry that I was unable to shed one tear, acting as if his lash didn't faze me. I looked up at him and mumbled, "No, I'm going!"

Not expecting that response from me, Tyrone speeded away down Bel Air Road, turning corners as if we were on train rails. Shortly thereafter, we emerged in front of a house, 1701 Richardson Ave. All I could do was think to myself and how much I hated this house and everyone in it, and I meant everyone in it. Watching out the window at the brick row house made me so overwhelmed with emotion, I could still feel stinging on my face and my flesh getting hot to the touch. While sliding my hands across my cheek, I could feel one ridge, then two ridges, then a third ridge. I realized that Tyrone had managed to imprint his whole handprint on my face. The tears found their way down my cheeks suddenly hearing the truck door slam and Tyrone say, "I'll be back and don't turn on my car!" Prompted me to glance over at the ignition to observe that he had taken the keys anyway, leaving me in the truck. On a fall night with no way to turn the heat on. By this time, it was in the low 50's, maybe even 40 degrees. Early morning weather. I sat there in the passenger seat, reflecting on my life and the choices I had made, asking myself questions like, why me? Why am I staying with this man? What type of hold does he have over me? How long was he going to be in there? I fell deeper and deeper into my thoughts. I never realized that I had drifted off to sleep. I could still feel the coldness of the wind from the open window dancing on the remaining tears that we're now drying up on my cheeks. I slowly relaxed my body and I drifted to sleep.

 I could hear the chime of the ignition beeping as the key inserted into the ignition. Hearing that engine crank up prompted me to open my eyes.

Opening my eyes felt like a task since they felt heavy from all the crying and the abuse they had taken hours before. I couldn't lie. Candy was right when she said I had gotten what I'd asked for, but what? Once open and now focusing, I was immediately drawn to the dashboard where in bright green numbers the time was displayed and reading 7:08 AM. Not believing that this could be right, I sat up in the passenger seat that was laid back in a reclining position for more comfort.

I turned to the right and the left for confirmation that I was still where I thought I was. It couldn't be true, but it was. I had spent the night in front of 1701 Richardson Ave. Tony's house. Tyrone's baby's mother's house. While trying to make some sense of this. I hear a faint voice in my ear rise and shine killer. He was chiper and unbothered. Taken back by the blatant disrespect, but not surprise, I simply said. "What did you say?"

And in an even clearer voice, Tyrone leaned over. The center console and says to me, "Good morning baby!"

Before I could even respond he planted a kiss solid on my lips that was completely out of the normal since Tyrone and I never, not even during sex, kissed in the mouth. And what made it even weirder was the fact that in the four seconds it took for him to kiss me, I could smell. The residue from his early morning activities and most likely the reason we had come to this house in the first place.

After taking a glance in the back seat. I realized that my conclusions were right. Since Jewel was not in her car seat and we were now pulling away from her mother's house, I retained this information like a sponge. I must admit, though, it was a gut punch I was drowning inside. My heart began to race. My mouth became dry. I could even feel my blood pressure rising. To what doctors would consider a lethal level.

Keeping this in mind, I turned my body toward the driver seat and calmly whispered to Tyrone. "You fucked her, didn't you?"

The statement didn't move him a bit. After stopping at a red light, never letting his eyes come from off the road, he muttered. "Were you going to do it? With your drunk ***! My needs haven't changed and there always is someone that is willing to fulfill them, I keep telling you that. So, what you need to do is step your game up and don't be mad at me because you dropped the ball. Tend to your nigga and you wouldn't have these kind of problems."

Chuckling at his own statement, Tyrone laughed. Turn the music up and began to bopping to the music like he hadn't a care in the world. My jaw wanted to drop at his response, but it didn't nothing never, ever seem to amaze me anymore. It was sad but true. A man was always going to be a man. I just wanted him. I wanted him to know that I was just as crazy, if not crazier than him. For some reason I yearned for the respect of Tyrone. It was as if Tyrone and I were one of the same, so when giving him the eye and asking him to take me home, he knew exactly what I meant by it. Once we enter the doors to my house, my panties were around my ankles, and I was straddle over the arms of my brand new brown leather sofa from Rooms to go with my ass in the air. There was something about seeing wave patterns embark on my booty while sexing doggy style that enticed him. Every man could appreciate a good Big booty and Tyrone did oh, so well. See, that will be the first and the last time Tyrone would tell me that I'm not taking care of my business. I had the best pussy in Baltimore, according to many very satisfied men and women. And I took my title very seriously, so I was determined to make sure that he remembered exactly what an orgasm with Keisha Lorraine Stokes felt like. Yeah, she might have got him this time, but it wouldn't happen again. Not never again, Bitch.

Dear Diary, September 1st, 2010.

My mother always told me to never, ever let no female out here steal my man. You only let them get your leftovers, never the meat on your plate. I live by this, so anybody who steps to me better become ready for war.

Signed,
I'm ready!

Chapter 3

Alexis Nolan Washington.

"Yeah, baby, I know it's late. I'll be there in 20 minutes. I'm pulling off of Candy Street right now. I'm sorry, I will explain all about what's going on when I get... Hello. Hello. Hello." I can't believe he hung up on me.

Lord Desmond is going to flip out when I get there. Sitting at the light, I turned the radio up just to hear one of my favorite oldies but goodies songs playing on the Quiet Storm. Janet Jackson's *Funny how time flies when you're having fun*). Damn. I remember how Desmond and I had made love to the song the very first time we had sex. He was so gentle and patient with me. I believe I fell in love with that man while this song was playing. So how ironic that it was on the radio right now. I couldn't help but think how times have changed. Now we barely can be around each other for more than ten minutes without arguing about something. I guess that's why I cherish moments like these. Moments that allow me to remember why or how we fell in love in the first place. So, I sung and sung at the top of my lungs all the way home. Before I knew it, I was pulling my visor down to retrieve my garage opener. While the garage slowly rolled up and I made my way down our long driveway, I thought of how much I loved this house. I admired it and the presence it had in the community that was filled with such beautiful homes. It was definitely my dream house. The 20-foot ceilings in the foyer was home to the beautiful chandelier and an even bigger arch window. At night, the lights danced around on the 20-foot mirrors that surrounded it. It always has me in awe. No matter how many times I saw it, I felt so blessed to have my dream house and the family to go along with it. Sometimes I feel the need to remind myself of this. My husband worked overtime to provide us with a great life and that's exactly what we had.

But it was no secret that the beauty stopped at the door, since my husband and my relationship was not at its best. Beginning to remember the problems at hand, I reluctantly turned off my new BMW and turned to make sure the garage door had closed behind me. As I turned around, I noticed the door leading inside the house open abruptly, and before seeing him I could hear the angry military style bark come from Desmond. I think really sometimes that he forgot that I was his wife and not one of his soldiers. He could be so harsh sometimes. And his look, his look could intimidate even to the strongest. But I was his woman, and I knew him better than anyone. He wasn't gonna hurt me. Even if he thought he was scaring me with his tactics.

"Look, woman, I'm getting tired of this Bitch! Every time she called, you go running out of here like she's your woman or something."

Raising my eyebrow at him since Desmond tried his best not to curse. And, Bitch that was a harsh one. He never called women out their name. Part of why I fell in love with him. He was such a gentleman.

"If I didn't know better, I would say you and that girl were screwing."

"What, Desmond? Please give me a break! ****. If I didn't know you better, I would think that you were jealous of her!"

"So maybe you don't know me because I am."

Looking at him with a mean look I brushed off Desmond's remark, but not before asking him to repeat what he said. "What?"

"Then you don't know me at all! Why would you be jealous of a chick? I'm with you. You are my husband."

"I sleep in your bed every night, and that may be true, but she is the one you confide in and spend every waking moment with. She has you in ways I haven't had you in years. So yes, Alexis, I'm jealous!"

"Well, Desmond, if that's how you feel, you're crazy because it's not like that. And furthermore, she's my friend and I don't turn my back on my friends. You of all people should know that since that's one of the qualities you actually admired in me."

Underneath I did kind of know that he was speaking the truth, and I was neglecting my husband, well, really my family, by being with Candace so much. But this was my friend, and I was doing what any real friend would. Plus, there was no way I was going to say sorry to him now, after how the way he was talking to me, I was a stubborn person like that, and for some reason that's when he knew just the right buttons to push to bring that stubbornness out of me. With that in mind, any of my prior plans of apologizing to him had gone out the window.

Brushing past Desmond, who was now standing in the doorway with the player polo pajama pants that I had bought him for Father's Day on, having no shirt on, allowed me to admire how perfect my husband was. His *** were so perfect and arms. The muscles just bulged. His body was perfect. He was my own personal eye candy. Quickly snapping back out of it and getting over his gorgeous body, I entered the house. After seeing the pajama pants, I kind of knew what was troubling him. Since the only time he wore those was when he was planning something special for me. He knew how sexy I thought he looked in them and I could never resist him while he had them on. As I walked through the family room to the kitchen, I could see my youngest son fast asleep on my brother's sectional. So, I signaled Desmond to lower his voice and I decided to pretend to not know what the problem was and where the attitude was coming from no matter how hard he pushed. Plus, it was easier to do it this way because Desmond had a need to always be right and I was refusing to give him the satisfaction. Not today! I ignored Desmond's rude remarks and vulgar language as he continued to rant and rave. I went on putting away the groceries from earlier. Upon finishing cleaning the mess that was made in my absence by Desmond and the kids, I was even more annoyed. I picked up my baby boy and went up the stairs to put him to bed. I turned on his moon shaped night light and gave him his goodnight kiss that he is always so eager to get. Glancing back at the door to catch one last glimpse at him before shutting the door, I was so in love. I couldn't help but admire how precious he looked, all snuggled up in his blanket, with the night light perfectly hitting his handsome little face. I was truly honored to be a mom, even if I didn't act like it all the time. I was in love with my kids, and I knew they adored me as well. Fully aware of the saying that boys first love are their Mama I could feel how much my little man cared for me.

While walking down the hall, I made sure to check on my older son and kiss his little cheeks. Then finally entering our master suite where I just knew it would be a long night before I would be able to rest my eyes. Since I could tell from the persistence of Desmond that he would not be dropping the issue of Candace and my friendship anytime soon.

As soon as I had figured, I was fully prepared for Desmond's theatrics. I completed the entry to our master bedroom. I was taken back by the sight of fresh pink roses and the aroma of heavily scented candles I knew that scent anywhere they were. The Bath and Body Work Candles that he knew I loved. I could appreciate Desmond's attention to detail. I stood in front of the king size bed in amazement of the enormous amount of candles that were in there. Which had to have exceeded 100. And countless pink roses. I knew he had to have spent a small fortune on. This didn't surprise me because nothing was too much for Desmond when it came to me or the kids. I couldn't believe how clueless I had been of what the occasion was. It wasn't until I saw the big 10 And the life-size card near the window. Then realizing that there were 10 bouquets of my favorite flowers. Sunflowers! It was our ten-year anniversary and I had completely forgotten. I guess in all the drama. With my home girl I had let one of the most important days of the year slip my mind. Not even knowing what to say or even how to make up for the mishap, I was out of words. Only the tears and my face could tell the story of how awful I was feeling. I glanced over at Desmond to find him sitting on the edge of the brown oversized lounge chair that was in our room, staring out of the window into the woods. With a look of defeat on his face.

He didn't deserve the pain he was in right now, and the only person to blame was the same person that he would do anything in the world to make happy. And that person was me, just as I thought I had the words to say, Desmond said to me, "Lex, I can't and won't compete with any and everything you feel fit to put between us anymore. Today it's Candace, tomorrow is your work, and the next day is whatever else. I'm sick of it and I'm done pretending that it's not a problem."

"Baby?"

"Don't say nothing to me, Alexis. Let me finish," pausing for a few before speaking again. "Now you are the wonderful wife and mother when you are here. But the problem is you're never around anymore. I can't be comfortable having my wife hanging around females with the reputation those girls have. You are a gem to me but socializing with these people it's chipping away at my stone. It's not that it makes you any less beautiful. It is just that they're chipping away at all the beautiful things you have to offer making it less, and less you have to give to the people that value you the most. Don't you see, baby? The innocence that you once had and the purity is going away. You turn it into something I don't know or like for that matter. And the bad thing about it is that it's not you at all. All I'm asking you to do, Alexis, is come back to yourself. Be true to you. Don't be who you think everybody wants you to be. Be who you are and then see who was around. Then you will know who's for you and who's not."

I could see that he was speaking from the heart since he didn't lay an eye on me, not once, as if it would be too painful to do so. As I looked at him closer, I noticed he was crying. I was much too ashamed to look him in the eye. This was my husband. The person who I cared what impression he had of me the most?

I made sure he never caught me watching him finally turning towards me. I could see his face was full of tears and his emotions showed all over his body. He was hurt deeply. Once again, I was at a loss for words, but I knew the time drew near for me to have to speak and explain the way I had been acting. He got up from where he had been sitting and started to come closer to me and for some odd reason, I grew more and more nervous with every step he took. All kinds of thoughts filled my mind, saying a little prayer. Lord, please don't let this man hit me. He was right in front of me by this time, grabbing my hands and looking into my eyes. He said to me, "Alexis, I don't know what to do. I see you, the person I love most in the world, turn into everything I hate right before my eyes, and I can't do anything about it. All I can do is fight for you and pray that the person I fell in love with will come back to me because I'm here waiting for her. I will never give up on you, but eventually I will stop fighting for you. I love you, baby. But the street life and these girls are not for you. They're going to make you distant everything, including your husband and your family."

With his last words, he left the room, leaving me with so many questions and even more responses. I couldn't find the words to get out while he was right in front of me, but now I just wanted to blurt them out. Just to give him some clarity so that he could know that I wasn't trying to neglect my family and I do care for his feelings most of all. I loved him more than anything as well, but he was already gone, and my time had passed to voice my side of things. All I was left with was a heart full of emotion and one very lonely yet beautiful master suite.

The next morning, the house was routinely busy. The smell of hot coffee. In the air last minute wardrobe changes for the kids as well as Desmond and I was going over the schedule of who was going to do what during the week. The kids always tried to sneak peeks of Sponge Bob before leaving out, which made them extra slow when putting their clothes on. This drove me crazy to no end, but it was what I had been accustomed to and would have it no other way. I thought long and hard of the events from last night. And the thought of any of this changing made me visibly sad. Vouching not to dwell on the past, I focused my attention on the present, almost nearing the time for TJ, my oldest son, to get on the bus, which was the same time I left to take my baby boy to daycare. The race against the clock began and the house became even more chaotic as I approached the door to walk TJ to the bus and put the baby and my things in the car. I found Desmond sitting on the steps leading to the outside. Startled by him, I jumped, "Boy, you scared me." Then regaining my composure quickly. "OK baby, I'm leaving." I headed straight toward The car. I was stopped in my tracks by a low yet stern voice saying, "Alexis, we can't keep doing this!"

Knowing exactly what he was referring to, I just continued my steps toward the car. "And yeah. I love you, sweetie." By now pulling the door to the car shut behind me. As I reversed out the driveway, I could feel something looking at me. Once at the end of the driveway, I took one last look at the house. To my relief, I wasn't going crazy by feeling as if someone had been looking at me. It was indeed Desmond peeking out the blinds from in the living room window. Seeing him and now catching his eyes staring back at me, my husband and I shared a moment. A moment where I felt his pain and at that very moment, I knew my marriage was in jeopardy. Last night, Desmond shift seemed angry. Today, the ora was different.

He was tired. With only a short pause and just barely a chance to change gears, the kids and I were off.

After I dropped my son off to school, I was again all wrapped up in my thoughts. It was starting to become a normal thing for me, speaking to myself. Since I could never find a word to speak to my husband, who was what I consider to be my best friend. As for my friends who I knew couldn't relate to what I was going through, they were all unmarried and their ideas of problems were who was going to wear what to the club? I was lonely in my thoughts. I tried to convince myself that the feelings I was having would pass eventually, because I had too much on my plate to have to deal with an insecure man. But was he insecure? Or was it that I was not being a good wife? With that, I had settled the issue in my opinion, and I was free to start my day. I was a bad wife bottom line, I needed to do better. I knew what I had to do but it couldn't happen now. I had zoned out. Not even realizing that I had finally pulled up to the concrete building. Just as I got there, I remembered why it was that I hated coming out to this office in Glen Burnie so much. It always seemed to remind me that I wasn't normal and maybe trying to pretend to be. I was indeed handicapped. I parked the car in the handicapped spot right next to a girl I had remembered from my last visit here. What a coincidence since that was almost two months ago. She was a cute girl, but she always seemed to look so sad, staying in the car until she left. I watched her limp into the office, and I thought to myself is that how I look when I walk? Giving her enough time to get off the long walkway without any interruption. She had gone into the building. Following not too far behind was three or four people, I assume, was her family. I finally got out of the car, slamming the door behind me, and proceeding to start my stroll into the building. Once inside I could see there were about four people waiting to be seen ahead of me. After I gave my name to the receptionist, I took my seat in the waiting area. For some reason it was always uncomfortable in this place. Everyone stared at each other like you were from another species. Trying to figure the next person out. All I could think was could this man please hurry up and call me to the back. I was so ready to go, but I waited patiently. 10 minutes and two Fall inspired magazines later, I was called to the back for Mr. Cohn.

I quickly rose to my feet when he called me. I could feel four sets of eyes on me, but I didn't care. However, I did make sure every step was perfect to the best of my ability. Mr. Cohn escorted me to the back office and to my examination room. I was relieved to be out of there finally. He led me to a cold room with all white walls and all kinds of mechanical machines that I couldn't help but wonder what they all did.

As I sat down on the examination table, I didn't even realize that I had said it's stunk in here, out loud. Mr. Cohen explained that it was the materials that they used to plaster that left the scent in the air. It just wasn't pleasant, but it wasn't necessarily a bad smell either. Once we both were settled, I said to Mr. Cohen, "So what's that?"

I consider Mr. Cohen, like a friend rather than a doctor. I mean, he had been with me for a very long time making my prosthesis.
"I'm good," he said. "And yourself"

"I'm good, but I am having some problems with my leg." I went on to tell him that it felt like the leg he had made for me was now too small. It was tight and uncomfortable. It even pinched sometimes. I always had a blister, but I never let it get in my way. After all, I did just have a baby not too long ago, so there was some baby weight that was causing the discomfort. Not being able to walk well with my prosthesis really bothered me. It was annoying to be very honest. I just hated walking with a limp, always having one leg looked at as handicapped. For some reason, Candace thought I was born with a birth defect. I had never told her that, but truthfully, Candace never asked what happened to me. She always acted like she didn't see my leg or that I had a problem. In some ways it was a good thing, but not all the time. I know it was partially my fault, since I didn't make it clear to her, indeed, that I was an amputee. I always treated it as a not to know basis. This condition that she referred to as a defect was really a result of childhood cancer. I guess I was just too in love with the idea of being looked upon as a normal woman versus a handicapped one. I just wanted people to believe that I was normal. I didn't want anyone to hear my sad story and befriend me out of pity. That's another whole story.

I was here at the doctor's office, and I needed my prosthesis fixed ASAP. Really Mr. Cohen wasn't considered to be a doctor. He was actually called a prosthetist, but never mind the formalities. After taking my leg off and further examining it, Mr. Cohen found a way to fix the problem. He assured me that he would have me out of there in plenty of time to do all the many errands I needed to run. Most importantly, before the kids got out of school and daycare. Finally finished and back in the car I thought about Candace and how uneasy I was becoming. I mean, I shouldn't be keeping secrets from my very good friend. She was my BFF. I was supposed to be able to tell her anything and everything. It was really crazy how over the years there had been plenty of stories of what exactly happened to me. Some were close to the truth; others were extremely far-fetched. It was amazing, and the fact that most had been started by Candace herself. She was creating my narrative. Never understood it, but never corrected her either. I wasn't sure if she would say these things just to shut people up or what, but I was truly realizing that I was really unhappy with being looked at as this mystery woman with the limp. This was my truth, and it was my story to tell. Why was I allowing her to create her own? She probably felt I had no backbone. Shit, I felt I didn't have any backbone. I was never scared of her, but only what she would think.

I made up my mind it was time for everyone to know the truth. It was gonna happen on my time and in my own way. The hard part would be finding when and where that place would be.

Chapter 4

Candace (Candy)

Shit, I have a headache. I thought to myself as I bent over one of the three kids that had sneaked into my bed while I was asleep. I had to move my son's head over in order to get the remote so that I could turn on the rerun of the Maury Show I missed last week. I knew that the paternity test filled episode. It would be great entertainment for my mind. It would help me get the events of last night out of my head. I knew that I needed to call Lexus since I had kind of snapped at her a little last night. She was really just showing genuine concern for me, how she acted like she cared for me more than my own Mama. I just didn't know how to take it really. I was just tired and irritated by everything that had been going on. Alexis just has a way of pushing all the wrong buttons. When I'm upset, she knows that I don't mean anything by it, however I felt the need to apologize anyway but not your traditional apology. We didn't do that. Or should I say I don't do that. I'm not saying sorry. I will call her which should surely reassure her that I wasn't angry anymore. Nah, I wasn't gonna say. sorry. That ain't even my style. Now Loretta, my Mama, she only cares about herself. I called her first before Tyrone to see if she could come and get me out of jail. I don't even know why I tried. See, crack took my mom from me years ago. Her drug addiction made my sister and my life, a living hell. We still are living with it. My Mama and her crack pipe are why I managed to have all these kids. I mean, I know that sounds crazy, but how was I supposed to survive at the age of ten with two sisters and no food or lights in a one-bedroom apartment? I was the oldest. She would leave us there for days. She wouldn't check on us, and when we needed her, it was too much hassle to go searching the 100 or so crack houses in our neighborhood that she frequently visited. What else was I supposed to do? I had to take matters in my own hands and do it for myself and my sisters. So, it became a normal thing for every bed that I was invited into I did just that, slept in it. Whether it was a man or woman, I didn't care. I think my first experience was actually with a woman. I had to have been like twelve. It's not really my thing, but if I had to do it I would. So that's why I call myself a survivor. There isn't much I wouldn't do to keep food on the table. That's just how I am. It's not such a bad trait to have if you ask me. I should really thank my momma for that. I would if I could, but I don't see her that often, which will be changing soon as my day rolls around for me to get my food stamps this week. Yeah, Loretta wasn't ashamed to let you know that she was using you. Her model was all of us get used by somebody at some point, so why hide it?

Picking up the phone, not even hesitating, I began to search my call log for Alexis's number. I didn't remember it by heart. Just as I got to the number and pressed the send to dial it, I looked up to see a strange figure jet past my bedroom door. With one swift movement, I dashed out the door, screaming to the top of my lungs. I know that's not who I think it is. By the time I got to the top of the stairs, I was face to face with Stevie. Stevie was the young hard headed boy that my 16-year-old daughter Taisha thought was the best thing since electronic food stamps. I couldn't stand him, and his father and I had screwed around a few times. I knew he wasn't cut from a good cloth. He was 19 years old and sold everything and every kind of drug on the street. I even heard he prostituted a couple of little girls around the neighborhood.

Since Taisha had the same attraction to money I did, I wasn't surprised to hear that he was buying her everything under the sun, and I knew that that was all she needed to stay locked in with this knucklehead. But I, of all people, knew what all those shopping sprees entitled her to have to do. I wasn't taking care of anybody else's babies, which would surely follow if Taisha continued seeing Stevie. Hell, I didn't want to take care of my own kids. Besides, what would he really see in her barely hitting puberty?! No hair having coochy, anyways? Taisha was what I called a late bloomer. Shit, I just showed the girl how to properly shave her under arms two days ago. Nigga, why the hell are you in my house at 9:30 AM in the morning?

"Stevie, did you stay here in my house?"

"I just came to see if I could borrow the clippers to cut my hair from Twin Miss Candace!"

Twin was my 17-year-old son.

"At this time of the morning, boy? You must think I'm stupid. I see you already have a haircut, Stevie. Boy, get the hell out of my house!"

"All right, that's what's up."

Lord, I hate this boy and the way he answered me made me want to hit him in his face. But I was on probation, and I couldn't afford any cops being called. I'm already scared because of what happened yesterday. That reminds me I need to figure out something to say just in case my probation officer calls.

All right, now I was focused and made a bee line to Taisha's room. I slowly opened the door to sneak up a glimpse of what she was doing before going off. I knew she would be taken back since she hadn't heard me catch Stevie coming from her room. After seeing Taisha looking out the window near the bed, I knew she was probably trying to catch one last glimpse at Stevie walking up the street to his house. Also, to see whether or not he would stop to go over one of his three babies' mother's houses. Her name was Tiny and she lived only a few houses down from ours which was in between our house and Stevie's. How ironic, this little asshole had

33

coochy on every block for about six blocks.

Back to focusing on Taisha's room on the side of the bed I noticed a half smoke blunt in a makeshift ashtray. Not too far from what, there were two empty bottles of Cisco and, on the floor, a new pair of my Victoria's Secret underwear. Seeing those put me in a rage. I was pissed off since I knew she had to have been searching my dresser drawer for them. Plus, I have been saving them for a special occasion. How dare she? Thinking to myself, this damn girl has lost her mind. After moving away from the window, I could see the anal beads and baby oil. What the hell did he have my baby doing? I can feel my stomach turning to think of what my child had been doing all night. From the looks of things, it was safe to say he had just taken Taisha 's virginity and made her into a woman doing very adult acts at 16. At least I thought she was a virgin. They use baby oil as lubricant. What a rocky move! Wow. She wasn't even worth buying some KY Jelly. My mind was spinning at the thought of the life she was headed for. Not being able to take it anymore, I barged into the room. Taisha damn near jumped out of her skin. Since from the looks of things, she was feeling like a woman. I know from experience. It's nothing like your Mama to bring you back to reality. I could see her convert into a little girl right before my eyes. Stuttering my name. Taisha yelled out. "Mammmma" and she began to back up into the wall. The next time I catch that boy in my house, your ASS is out of here! Moving closer with every word I quickly immersed nose to nose with my child, so close that it revealed freckles that I never knew she even had on her face. I could feel the fear, not to mention see it all over her.

"I am your mother and I wish you would not be in my house and smoke, drink, and screw some boy in here disrespecting me. You are a child, and you will stay in your place in my house." I could see the tears swelling up in her eyes. In fear of what I would do next, I had to leave the room and it was best that I did so now. I always feared my own temper since it was bad, really bad! For some reason, I couldn't control myself when I was enraged, and I knew that I would hurt her really bad if I if I put my hands on her. See, this wasn't Taisha's first time. I had to get in her face before. The last time things went a little bit different though, since it resulted in me having to bail myself out of jail and spend another six months trying to get CPS to release her back into my custody. I was actually grateful since I heard this could take a long time. But in my case, I had a really good caseworker as she understood it was hard raising teenagers. I don't take any masks from my children, but I still love them, and I was trying my hardest to be a better mother than the one I had. I just couldn't accept disrespect. Not from them, not from no one, under no circumstances. Vowing to myself that if I was given another chance with my daughter, I would never resort to that kind of violence again, but there was no need for those desperate measures this time because I could see the shame and disappointment on her still naked body. I hadn't even given her an opportunity to put her clothes on. After looking at her, I couldn't help but think about how she will be paying for her indiscretion when she takes a bowel movement in the morning. That not so lubricated lube burns when coming out, I should know!

With that, I turned and headed down the hall to my room. I could feel her eyes piercing my back, so I turned and gave her one last stern look in disgust. Finally, I was back in my room. I shut the door and sat on the edge of the bed. Something came over me. I began to pray for my children and their future. I felt like a failure as a mother, but I didn't know how to do better. I asked God to guide me and walk with me so that I could steer them in the right direction. I knew without the power of prayer my babies were going to be taken by the streets. I was a very spiritual person. I did grow up to believe that there was a God, and I truly was a believer. My grandma made sure that we stayed prayed up when we would see her on the weekends as a little girl. I think she knew that we needed it since our lives were very different from many others our age. Grandma always wanted to take us in, but she was way too old to keep up with us, girls. So, we stayed with our Mama and we visited grandma regularly. After she died, I kind of gave up on God. I was angry that He had taken away the only constant in my life. But once I had kids, I knew that the only way I could be a good mother would be to get God back into my life. So, I pray. I pray all the time. I pray every day and I leave them in his hands since I'm not the right person for the job, clearly. I can't even get my **** straight.

While I made the bed up and began to take out my clothes, I could hear my phone ringing. I really wasn't in the mood for any talking today, but I didn't want to be out of the loop when it came to what was going on with everybody, so I opted to answer the phone. What? Still a little angry and displaying it in my voice. What the **** is wrong with you? I've been calling you all day! I'm on my way over there. For what? Feeling even sicker to my stomach, I reluctantly said okay and hung up the phone. It was House. A dude I had met a few months ago at an after-hours spot. House was an okay guy. He tends to be very generous with his money, but he lacked any skills in the bedroom. I wonder about him because he seems to me that he may have been gay. I knew all about that download stuff and baby, I am not with it. I can't be a part of no double life. But the money that he gave me was too good to risk losing it and being wrong. And besides, I did need my hair and nails done, so I guess I'm due. After that fight last night, I'm in desperate need to get all my stuff done, so I gave myself a little pep talk and went straight to the shower. Putting on one of my cutest outfits, I was ready for House. I was actually getting kind of horny to be honest. I was ready for him to come and take advantage of all my assets. Some may call this prostitution shit, My bills needed to be paid, so I called it compensation. I never understood why I felt the need to have to validate how I took care of myself and my children, in people's eyes. They may call me a hoe, but I call it surviving.

My phone was ringing again. This time I actually wanted to answer it. I picked up the phone to see a picture of House on the screen.

This man was fine though I could never take that from him. He had long locs and a medium brown complexion. His hair was jet black and his eyes were just the right shade of brown, If you looked at them in the light, they even looked Hazel at times. Damn, his Mama m a d e a masterpiece. One thing I could do was appreciate a Fine Black man! His arms and abs were to die for. I love watching him, so much so I would find myself dazing off while looking at him exploring every inch of his body with my eyes. It was always embarrassing when House would catch me watching him. He probably felt I was weird or something... I mean, any woman in their right mind would drop their drawers for him. I began thinking to myself, I really hope that that five years in prison didn't have him liking the doodoo shoot. Laughing to myself, I looked at the picture of my phone until the screen changed to black. Dang, I had missed his call. Just as I was about to put the phone down, a text came through reading "ANSWER THE DOOR!" after slightly shaking my head. I rose to my feet and began down the stairs to the front door. Just as my foot hit this last step, I heard a loud popping sound coming from outside. I recognized the sound and dropped to the ground. I was all too familiar with the dreadful sounds of gunshots. I grew up around them all day, every day. My sisters and I would always say gunshot, gunshot. In the city they were our equivalent to birds chirping in the county The suburbs.

After about the sixth shot, everything went silent. It was now over but immediately I focused my attention on the door. Where was House? Growing more and more concerned my fear turned to panic as I approached the door and unlocked it. Finally, hearing police sirens sounding like music to my ears. Since mostly all the time, this meant that it was safe to go and be nosey.

Now swinging the door open, to see if House was there. He wasn't! But is there a coincidence that my whole block was in the middle of the street, crowding around a large figure? Not being able to see the person lying in the street my mind began to fill with negative thoughts. Who could this person be? Oh Lord, please don't let it be House. I walked quicker and quicker into the middle of the street. The crowd began to get bigger. I felt myself walking close to get the look of the body. My mouth began to feel dry, and my palms began to sweat. Just as I got about 10 feet from the body searching for a clear view, I felt a arm quickly surround my neck. A voice whispered in my ear, "Baby, you don't want to see that!" My body instantly got weak since I recognized the voice to be House. He was okay and I was for sure that I had just had a panic attack. I had just gone through every emotion within the last five minutes. The tears began to flow as my body became more and more relaxed. Seeing how I was worked up, I was visibly touched by House. "Ah, baby, you love me, huh?" He looked at my expression and could see that I wasn't in any mood for any jokes? With that, he just walked me over to the front door, almost having to carry me the whole time. Finally getting my composure after sitting on the steps for a while, I found my words and lashed out at how I thought that was you. I thought you were dead. He kissed me on the forehead and said, "Nah baby, I'm cool."

With that out the way, it was time to round up my kids, who were now all outside gossiping with the neighbors who were putting their spin on what they thought had happened and to who this mystery man was that was in the middle of our street. The crowd had grown so big the police couldn't even get to rope off the area before what looked like his family had arrived. By the time I had managed to get all the kids to the house there were detectives everywhere, which always meant it was time to go. Since they would surely be wanting to ask questions to whomever would answer. And like we said, in my neighborhood, snitches get stitches! That was definitely a no no. Around here snitching was the fastest way to get a one-way ride to the morgue. I remember sometimes as a little child my friends were told to look out at the crime scenes by the dope boys around the block, they were paying them $10 to watch and see who was talking to the cops. Not too long after, we would hear of the people that were snitching. We would then hear of them being killed or missing, sometimes we would even hear of their homes catching fire unexpectedly. The girls would even get gang raped as a lesson which they would most times wish they were dead due to the shame of showing their faces around the block. I was always told to keep every and anything to myself and that's how I raised my children. Being as though asking questions or even knowing too much was never a good thing.

Once we all got inside, I turned to lock the door. It was usually open all day since the children were in and out so much, but today was not one of those days. I wouldn't be letting them go outside, there was just too much going on and nerves were shot! I walked up stairs to find my 11-month-old and 3-year-old still sleeping. That was a relief; I knew that there would be no way I could deal with them right now. I left out the room to go to the bathroom so I could splash some water on my face and "woosa" I had taken that from one of Martin Lawrence films and it really worked for me. While I was in the bathroom which I shared a wall with my son's bedroom, I could hear Twin tell his sister that the boy in the street was Damon Cook who was the brother of one of my daughter's friends! All I could do was shake my head and continue on washing up. That news was going to raise a whole other issue since I know my daughter Lisa is very sensitive person and she was sure to take this news hard. When finally finished I came out of the bathroom into the hall. Twin's room drew completely silent. Apparently, they were attempting to have a private conversation. So, I walked by the room never letting on that I had heard everything. Just as I down the steps at the end of the hall I yelled out toward Twin bedroom "and yawl better stay out of it too! "We Will!! In unsung the replied screaming back at me. It wasn't easy raising kids in this area in Baltimore City. There were endless illegal things for them to get into where another child from the county may have had to get on a bus or drive to find. Our kids just had to walk out the front door and it was there. But this was the best I could do with the money I got from social services. My section eight vouchers had been revoked for having too many people living in my house, so I ended up here.

Almost forgetting I had company I went into the kitchen to find House rolling up a blunt at the kitchen table. Taken back by the site, I stopped and looked at him like he was crazy.

"What?"

"What you mean what fool? You do know I have children in this house, right? Not to mention they are up, and I don't smoke in front of them."

"Yeah, yeah, yeah, yeah. My bad. Sorry, I was just rolling up. I assume since I was downstairs. I was good. Okay!"

"Well, don't assume ****."

"Candy, I wasn't going to Light it damn!"

"Boy, you are lying. Yes, you were. Anyway, go down into the basement and smoke and make sure you close the door. My son has asthma."

"Cool, that's what's up. Are you smoking with me?"

"I don't know. I'll be down there after I get the kids some cereal." By now the little ones were up and they were hungry.

All I could think of is damn, I hate going down to that basement. It was so gloomy. Plus, there were a lot of cobwebs and roaches crawling around spiders and everything else you could think of. I hate it. **** that crawl. The air tends to be cold, and it smelled like a sweaty gym that got flooded. But after the last 48 hours (about 2 days), I needed some weed. **** I deserve some sex, all the hell I done been through.... So, with that I decided to get the kids together and send them over to my sister's house. It was just a short walk so this was perfect. Now it was time to have adult time. All I had to do was open the door to the basement to get my first contact. It was an overwhelming smell of Kush. So, it wasn't a surprise to not get a whiff of that awful b a s e m e n t smell. With every drag from House's freshly rolled blunt the very high quality marijuana, I began to feel more and more relaxed. This stuff was good, and I was high ****. I was stuck like I like to say. At this point, not even the very large spider that landed on my arm was bothering me. I just brushed it off and laughed about it. House noticing that I was feeling it, and my guard was down, he began rubbing all over my booty and squeezing my *** cheeks the best way he could since it was way too big for him to grip only with one hand. I always kept in mind that my big round booty that most men compared to Buffy the body was an asset. I was never to devalue myself anyway. If you wanted a piece of me, you had to pay for it, and I wasn't ashamed to say so. Girls out here would kill for a body like mine, and I knew it. Women envied me and my aunt drove men crazy, and House was no exception with this in mind. I played my part acting like he was the most irresistible sexiest man in the world making sure he was good and aroused, judging from the size of the bulging side of his very fly brand-new pair of Affliction jeans. This will be the perfect time to put a stop to things and remind him so he can retrieve my funds. I'm about my coins, and not even a good sex session was going to cloud my judgement when it came to that.

Still holding a handful of my ass, House began to kiss all over my chest, moving upward to my neck and slowly traveling to my lips. I turned my head, quickly changing the course of his travels. I didn't believe in kissing on the lips, to just anyone. It was way too personal for me. I wanted to save my passionate kiss for the one I married. You can say it's just my little idiosyncrasy. Feeling the mood changing into one that would very soon become intimate. I pushed House off of me and stood back away from him. So, he could see all the body which he wanted so badly while I said my peace. Pure desperation and confusion showed all over his face. Reaching out to me to pull me closer, House began mumbling. "Baby, what's wrong?" I rolled my eyes.

"I want you, girl. Stop playing and get over here."

I had House right where I wanted him.

"Candace, what are you doing?"

I lashed back at him. "You got the wrong Bitch! Where's my money?"

"Damn, I got you. You can have whatever." Whatever, My ears perked up to hear that word.

"Yeah man, whatever you want. Just get over here and drop them drawers."

Laughing out loud, It was kind of funny to me because while I was watching him talk it kind of looked like he was drooling at the mouth. Making the saying 'all men's are dogs kind of ring true,' or at least act like them.

"See, Why are you playing?"

Here, since you don't believe me, adjusting his aroused penis before digging into the hooping shorts he had on underneath his jeans, he pulled out three rubber bands, bound knots of money. My mouth dropped at the sight of all that money. I knew he didn't lack in the money department, but I never ever seen that much money on anyone person before. He handed me one whole cluster, confused, unsure if he was just telling me to hold it or giving me the whole thing. I asked him how much is it?

"Look more than enough."

"Now get over here and give me some of that pussy!"

I was more than willing to oblige since the sight of money turned me on to not being able to control my own excitement. The energy filled eight minutes of sex was surprisingly pleasurable.

Once back upstairs, House jaded passed me to go to the bathroom, so I just started toward my room. I was glad it was over, but I was even happier for the money. I wish he would hurry up and leave. Before he could regain his senses and asked me for some of the money back. Because it would definitely be a fight in here today. I had a No Refund policy. When in the room I began to gather my personal so I could take a shower, but the curiosity was killing me. I had to know how much money he gave me. I pulled it out from in my bra under my breast and started counting 20 after 20 after $20 bills, I could hear House coming up the hallway. He came into the room and plopped himself onto the bed, looking at me in what seemed like in amazement, he said to me. I sure love that ass of yours. I shall love this money you got. Still counting, I had finished to see he had given me $200, short of $1000 dollars. Watching my expressions once I was done, he said, "Well, you good?"

"Yeah, I guess!"

"What you mean you guess? I mean, I'm just saying you might as well give me the $200 and make it an even $1000.

"YOU aren't ever satisfied!"

His words got under my skin. "And you are? We both know that you will be right back here two days from now, wanting some more pussy. Why should I act satisfied?"

I could see that argument was brewing, so I just escorted House to the door. As I shut the door behind me. I screamed out YES! I had another successful day at the office. And off to the shower I went. Making a mental note not to forget to call Lexus and that Nico had said he would be coming home from off the road tonight. With that in mind. I would need to get cleaned up and out of the house fast. The last thing I wanted to do was have sex with my old man tonight.

Chapter 5

Keisha

I got up and out this morning. I didn't want to stay laid up under Tyrone today. Couldn't tell from last night that I would act like this, this morning. But his little trip to his baby mother's house really got under my skin. It was one thing for him to have a baby with what was supposed to be his jump off. (Chick on the side) That he cheated with two years ago when we were going through our drama. But it was another thing to still be sleeping with the girl and flaunting it in my face. He always says he doesn't want to hide anything from me, some **** about him wanting me to feel secure in our relationship. How the hell can I do that when he's screwing every female out here in my face? If that ***** could read, I would swear he read some kind of psychology book on how to control and manipulate people.

I keep my hair, nails and my feet done. I stay with new clothes on. I'm always up on what's new in style and fashion trends. Sexually, I do whatever whenever he wants me to. Even letting him have threesomes with two other girls, not even taking part in them most of the time. What other women could he find that would let their man do that? I do realize that I am a little heavier than he might want me to be, but I'm working on that. Sometimes, I just start feeling sorry for myself because I try and try but nothing seems to be working. Yet and still, I have to be happy because at least I had someone to call my own. Even if he doesn't love me the way I would like him to. **** it's hard out here by yourself. I needed help so why not get some much needed help and fill my bed at the same time? I mean, I knew he was in someone else's panties every chance he got, but he still laid in my bed every night for the most part.

Damn, I hated having to give myself these little pep t a l k s . They were happening more and more these days, which may be a clear sign that I was getting tired of Tyrone's bullshit. I already knew that he was the worst kind of guy to have, but it was just better than the alternative to me. I'm the kind of girl a relationship expert would call needy when it comes to a man. If you ask anyone who knows me, they will say I treat everyone like shit but a man. I give them my all and then some. It's just how I am. I compromised everything for him. I loved him and that's all it was. But this morning I just needed a little time to remind myself of why it was that I was in love with Tyrone. I was so hurt. This time he had gone too far. I normally was really good at convincing myself that I was the reason for him acting out, but for whatever reason it wasn't working today. So, after about eight bus stops and one train ride out to BWI Airport, I was back downtown. I had to go to my aunt's house out Laurel for the night to clear my head. Right before exiting the train, I came to the realization that it had to be my disrespectful mouth and lack of weight loss that had pushed him into those other girls' beds, coming to the conclusion in time. It prompted me to go into the mall and buy my baby a 'I'm sorry, gift.' It was my last bit of money for the month that I had planned on using for some food for my girls to eat in the upcoming week. But pleasing, Ty was more important to me at the moment. Besides, I could always send them down to my grandparents' house after school to eat. Plus, there was some cereal in the house, I could just get one of them to pick up some milk, convincing myself that the girls would be fine. I made my way into the mall. Searching around for a few, I managed to find the Philly fitted Hat, that Tyrone had been wanting and a nice outfit to go along with it. I'm not so happy about the amount of money I spent though. FUCK IT! Left with only $5 to my n a m e until next Friday would be a ***** I thought to myself. But I was way too excited about the gift I bought Tyrone to worry about that now. This was sure to have been the best apology gift I had ever gotten him, and Lord knows there have been a few.

It was now around 12:00 in the afternoon, so I knew I should be getting a call from Tehran or the girls soon looking for me. I would need to start the walk home now if I was going to be there before they left out. Walking was the only option now since I had was broke, and only had $5, it wouldn't be enough to get a cab ride home. Nor a hack. I mean, six blocks shouldn't be that bad, I thought to myself. It would be like my first day of working out with each block, my excitement grew more and more on how my man would respond to my peace offering. An hour later, I was finally home. To my surprise, the girls had already gone, and Tyrone was still sleep. That was great, because it gave me the opportunity to whip Tyrone up one of his favorite breakfast sandwiches. Since the girls were already gone, I knew I wouldn't be seeing them until the evening sometime and at 11. At 13 they weren't babies, so it was fine for me. More time for me to give to my man. I made sure the girls went to the clinic on a regular basis, and I always stayed with a supply of condoms. I wasn't dealing with any babies, supporting them, or even having them in my house. I was done with raising kids. Hell, if it wasn't for it being the law, I would have already put them bitches out of my house. But since they were here, and I had to have them in my house utilizing the system and get some money was what it was going to be. Child support, welfare, something for them being here, cramping my style. Do they know what I could be doing if they weren't around? I looked at it as them earning their keep. Nothing was for free.

"Baby, baby, baby, get up. I got your breakfast." Tyrone was balled up in the blanket in a fetal position, mouth wide open and sweating like he had just ran a marathon. I must have startled him when I woke him because he jumped up with his 357 Magnum in his hand. He had a puzzled look on his face that made me believe he wasn't all the way awake yet and if I didn't do something fast, he would shoot any second. So, I identified myself, making sure not to speak too loud and further startle him. I said, "Baby, it's me Keisha. Put the gun down." I was shaken! By now, a little more alert now.

Tyrone's eyes were now focusing on me. Putting the gun down he laid back down on the bed and began to scream at me. "Girl, how many times I have to tell you to stop waking me up. Your ***** can wait until I wake up. For whatever you want, you're going to get your ******* killed messing with me in my sleep. If the house isn't on fire, don't wake me up."

Okay, okay it was my fault. I had forgotten to put his gun away before I woke him up. I usually always looked for it before bothering him when he was sleep. I h a d learned my lesson after he had shot at me and grazed my shoulder a few years ago. "I forgot. Baby, I'm sorry but here is your food."

"What is it?"

"A breakfast sandwich with bacon and eggs. A slice of scrapple on toasted bread with butter and jelly. Oh, and a glass of Tropical Punch, Kool-Aid on the side." He loves it that way.

"Where is the apple sauce?"

Damn it, I forgot. I'll go and get it for him now. Up and eating, I went to get his applesauce and gift I had just bought him. By the time I returned to the room, most of his food was gone and the TV was on Sports Center. He was playing a new mix rap song. Not able to hear myself say a thing, I said, "Here you go." I handed him the bowl and the bags. Tyrone snatched them out my hands, not even acknowledging or at least saying thank you. He only continued to listen to his music while eating and watching highlights of last night's games. I had learned to g i v e him space when he was in moods like this one, so I backed off and decided to retreat downstairs. But before going, I made sure to grab the wet sheets off the bed. He always was wetting in them at night, so it was kind of the normal thing for me to do. You would think that bed wetting would be a shameful thing. To him a 27-year-old man, but it didn't seem to faze him in the least. He m e r e l y lifted up for me to get the sheets and proceeded to eat. It was time for me to watch my stories anyway. So, I went to the living room to watch TV. I needed a cigarette. Plus, I had not spoken to any of my girls today, so I decided to put in some calls as well. But one person call was way more important than anyone I would talk to today. I just had to call him. He was the one person who I knew I would need to meet up with before the day was over. That person w a s Nico. He is Candace's boyfriend who I have been sleeping with for about six months. After getting drunk and having a n unexpected threesome with him and Candace, we began seeing each other behind her back. I just had to get some of his *** to myself. We all had agreed to never sleep with each other again, but **** I lied. He just did stuff that I was not used to, and Candace wasn't riding that dick the right way anyway, from the performance she gave when we all got down. I just figured I'd do her the favor. If I didn't do it, another bitch would. I had never been with a guy who made love to me and enjoyed giving me pleasure while always asking me was it good and was I alright? Most Dudes I dealt with was all about self. I mean, if you didn't get yours before they did during sex, you was assed out. But Nico or Nek As I called him. He would always work overtime to make sure I was satisfied, and I loved it. His nice size muscular penis wasn't a bad bonus either. I didn't feel any guilt for sleeping with Candace's boyfriend. She should have never let me get a taste of him in the first place. If you ask me, it was her fault. She knew how I was and if I like something, I'm going to come back. I think that's why she would never bring him around me anymore after we did it. I couldn't help but flirt with him. He is just so damn fine. Sexy as hell, shit my panties got wet upon sight when I would see him. I sent a text out to him reading Maintenance, which he knew it meant for us to meet up at our normal spot after the club. It was a code so we wouldn't make any plans for the evening. Nico was an event planner and club promoter, so he was always out at all the hottest clubs and parties in Baltimore, DC, and Virginia. Pretty much, he ran the DMV. So, him not coming home or getting in real late sometimes, even getting a room, wasn't alarming to Candace. She could care less anyway since she was off doing her own thing most of the time. This gave him a lot of freedom that most guys that had women only dreamed of. Being the man that he was, Nico took full advantage of it. Candace, attention being off wherever it was, gave me the opportunity to be fulfilled by her man on a regular basis. I wasn't mad. There was only one problem, her nosey goody two shoes girlfriend, Alexis. I couldn't stand this *****. She was always in Candace's ear about how Nico was a good man, and she should treat him better, and how I was such a loser, and she should stop dealing with me. She could see right through me, but I didn't give a shit. What I did care about was how she was trying to get

Candace to change her ways and pay more attention to her man. See Candace was my little protege. She was just as or more fucked up than I was and for whatever reason, she looked up to me. So, I did what any woman in my position would do. I used her gullible ass to my advantage. I never kept anyone around me if I couldn't get something out of them. Anywhere from a ride to the store or a few $100. If you were around me, you served a purpose in my book. My motto was, why pay for it if you can get it for free? Candace was no exception. I needed her for Nico plus I wanted some money from the lead case settlement she was going to be getting really soon. That chick was too dumb to see me coming. See, as a child she lived in a home in Baltimore City that had lead paint. They tested her lead levels a few years back and they were really high and could contributed it to the house she grew up in with her grandmother. Crazy part is her grandma still stays there. The city had to pay out all the people who were affected by this and she is one of them. Where I come in is I told her that she could get money for living in there. I was the one that told her to go get tested. So, like I said she owes me, and I want my money from that settlement. Anyway, back to Alexis. She had her own secrets. No one could be that self-righteous without any skeletons in the closet. I just didn't know what they were. But I did know that she had to be a woman full of indiscretions.

Chapter 6

Alexis

I hated it when Desmond was upset. Just because I knew how much he just wanted the kids and me to be happy. I know no one could ever love me as much as he did, but for some reason I was always challenging his love for me. My phone rang when I was almost at the supermarket. It was Desmond checking on me. I answered, "Hey, sweetie."

"No, ***** I'm not your sweetie and I'm not your precious husband. That was who you thought it was, right? Or are you finally letting another nigga tap that ass?"

I couldn't help but laugh at that foolish Candace. The way she said things kept me in stitches. "Whatever, Candace. Yes, I did think you were my husband. I'm expecting his call. I'm at the market. So, what's up?" Candace and I had a weird friendship. We never spoke about our problems with each other. We would just go on like nothing ever happened. It didn't shock me that she didn't mention or even allude to our little disagreement the other night.

"Well, Lex girl. You wouldn't believe the morning I've been having. Besides finding that sorry as little boy Stevie trying to sneak out my house at 8:00 in the morning. House came by, but they were shooting when he got out here. I thought it was his *** that got shot."

"OMG! Was he OK?"

"Girl bye. Yeah, he's good girl. But you know what he wanted, right?"

"Yeah. So, the minute man strikes again, huh?" Laughing at what she had just stated. I had to ask, "So what did you do?"

"BITCH, What you think I did? Got my money."

"Wow, Candace, how much did you get this time?"

"About $1000."

"What? Damn, what you turn into a Hoover? **** that's enough to make me get a little jump off. No, I'm just joking. But seriously, you need to stop cheating on Nico like that. He's good to you."

"Nico is my baby, don't get me wrong, but I'm not going to be a fool and think he is not messing with chicks at all these parties. At the end of the day, he is a man."

"True Candy, and I'm not saying you need to be a fool, but all I'm saying is don't hurt him and he doesn't deserve it. All these years that he has been doing promotion, you have never heard of any females he was supposed to be with. With a job like that in Baltimore, being as small as it is, you would have seen or heard something by now. If he has been cheating he is a damn good one or the person he's cheating with got a lot to lose to by getting caught. Just think of how you would feel if the roles were reversed."

After making that last statement, my phone b e e p e d and this time it really was Desmond. He wanted to check on me and how my doctor's appointment went. Interrupting Candace, I had to abruptly end our conversation, So that I could take the call from my hubby. I could hear the frustration in Candie's voice when I told her I would have to call her back. I was rushing to click over to the other line before missing his call, not even saying bye to Candace, or waiting for her to acknowledge what I had said. Desmond was funny like that. He tends to get upset if I didn't pick up the phone or left him on hold for too long. Considering the fact that we were already on shaky ground, I didn't need any additional problems. So, in a very unmoving soft tone I said, "hey." I could hear a lot of noise in the background which quickly answered my next question if he did go to work? Sorry to say it, but I was kind of relieved. Because I didn't want to argue more with him when I returned home from the market, which I was almost positive would happened since I was aware that he had only skimmed the surface of our problems last night.

With a stern voice, Desmond asked, "So how did it go?"
Desmond sounded as equally unmoved as I did.

"Everything went fine. Thanks for asking."

"That's good, sweetie. Where are you?"
"I'm at the market picking up some things for dinner. I think I will go home and take a nap when I leave before the kids get home. What would you like to eat tonight for dinner? I was thinking steak and shrimp. You know the way you like it with mashed potatoes and broccoli."

"That sounds good," he replied.

I was trying to avoid at all costs any mention of last night and our anniversary. I was almost cleared. All I needed to do now was get him off the phone. Desmond wasn't an easy person to divert. When he had his mind made-up, he was extremely persistent and strong minded. The mood on the phone call was really awkward and the long silence pause made the moment even more awkward. The conversation felt like it was about to change, so this would be the time for me to exit the phone before things change. I said, "Well honey, I'll talk to you later."

To my surprise, he simply said, "Okay." Then he informed me of his plans on leaving work early to come home and have lunch with me. It was a nice gesture, but I couldn't stop wondering why he wanted to come home in the first place. I guess I would have to just find out.

Thirty grocery bags later I was home and Desmond met me there, so I had help with all the bags, which I was relieved about. Tired, I couldn't wait to get in the house and change out of these uncomfortable clothing into my favorite PJ's, heading straight upstairs into my room to change. I had to return to the kitchen to put the groceries away and start on dinner. To my surprise, they had already been put away. There was a fire burning and two glasses of wine in our new Makisa crystal wine glasses when I returned to the kitchen. Floetry was playing in the background, so I was starting to feel the mood being set. Searching for Desmond, I found him in the family room just off the kitchen sitting on the arm of the sofa. "What is all this?"

He grabbed me by the arms and sat me down and said to me, "I'm sorry."

I wasn't expecting all of that. I mean, he was going back to work. I thought it was just lunch. My mind quickly started to wander. What, really, did he have to be sorry for? His words made me feel a little uncomfortable. He went on to say that he would get through things and how much he still and will always love me. So, with a kiss we sealed our apology and went on with our lovely afternoon after three wonderful glasses of wine and a great lunch with stimulating conversation, it was as if nothing had happened. I so love this man. And just like that, he was off back to work.

Later on that evening, I got a call from Candace saying that we should step out for a little bit. It was Thursday and it was ladies' night, which to me didn't seem like it was a bad idea being we both had been on a roller coaster ride in the last two days. Plus, I needed to talk to her. I had made-up my mind that I would be confessing to Candace that I hadn't been completely honest with her about my situation. I mean my leg. Although she got really emotional and sensitive when she was drunk. I thought that would be a perfect time so I was planning on breaking the news to her then. I had made up my mind. I left the house around 10:30 to go to the bar. We went to a local bar that kind of reminded me of the TV show Cheers. Since everybody did know everybody there, it wasn't that far from my house, so I didn't have far to travel back home. We started drinking some Patrone in the car, so by the time we got into the bar we were feeling good. When inside the bar, we got two glasses of Grey Goose and pineapple juice. We were sure to be really tipsy by the end of the night. I love coming to this place. The people were great, and we always had a great time. We were like neighborhood celebrities. We danced and played a little Spades. At about 12:00 PM, I was completely drunk. I didn't notice I had drunk so much until my head began spinning, so I knew it was time to sit down. I was done! Noticing how intoxicated I was, Candace called Desmond to come and get me once the bar let out, which made sense because she was gonna need a ride home herself. I had to use the bathroom, so once Candace's favorite Lil Wayne song went off, we both went to use the restroom. I began to vomit all the contents in my stomach, Old Bay wings and grey goose. Quickly trying to get myself together, the toilets all began to multiply by the threes. The girls all came in for a bathroom break. "Let's go!" Candace said. Candace did her best to pick me up and lead me outside to get some fresh air once getting me to the front door of the bathroom, Candace recruited one of her friends to help get me out of the bar. I swear that girl knows everybody. I just couldn't put one foot in front of the other for some reason. I could feel my prosthesis slipping off my body. I tried desperately to grab onto it, but I just couldn't. Between the sweat and my weak body, it was losing its grip. Slowly, it eased its way down my skirt and slid onto the floor. It felt like an out of body experience. I could feel everybody looking. I was instantly sober. The looks of amazement and confusion were overwhelming. It quickly turned into an explosion of laughter. Pointing and joking, instantly followed by an abruption of oh "SHITS" I felt as if I was a mouse in the middle of a whole pack of hyena. My world was all about to change for the worse, and I could see it. It took a little minute for Candace and her friend to notice what happened. Since they were so focused on getting me out of the bar. Once looking back, her friend was the first one to see. She instantly let go of me, causing the weight of my body to fall to one side. Feeling the absence of her friend, Candace turned to see the tears in my eyes and my leg about five feet away. Humiliation filled her face, and she dropped me free onto the floor. My body was so off balance it hit the ground hard and quickly. I was alone. A crowd of what seemed to me to be thousands surrounded me, and not one person offered a hand. Desperately I attempted to get to my prosthesis when I suddenly felt too strong, hands wisp me up and away into the air. Now being up so high allowed me to get a better visual of all the eyes piercing at me. Completely defenseless, I closed my eyes and allowed the stranger to usher me away. What felt like an extremely long walk across the parking lot. I was sitting in this stranger's car. Tears clouded my vision. All I could do was weep; I didn't even open my eyes to see that the car was moving. This person could be a kidnapper or rapist or a bad person for all I knew. I was just too upset to even care. As hard as I tried, I couldn't seem to regain my composure. There was absolutely no sound in the car. All I could hear was my weeping cry. It sounded. deafening and a little annoying even to me. The thought about who this person was or if he was a killer started to fill my head. This didn't even matter to me really. I was already dead at that moment in my mind. If you ask me, this was actually the best thing that could have happened to me, but it would be nice to see who this mystery person was. Suddenly the car stopped, and I knew this was it. I had left my mark on the world and God had finally called me home. I couldn't think of anything better to say to myself before whoever this man was, could kill me, but I would miss my kids. The only thing left to do was face the killer right as I got the nerves up to open my eyes. I heard the engine shut off. And what sounded like an angel's voice saying, "Alexis are you okay?"

How did he know my name? I wiped my tears and looked over to the driver's side seat. My vision was cloudy, but I could make out that it was Nico behind the wheel of the car. He was in a rather nice Cadillac Escalade. The sight of Nico caused my emotions to swell up again once again. By the time Nico extended his arms across the center console to console me I was a wreck of emotions once again, and in no condition to fight off his attempts to hold me. About twenty minutes of intense tears, screams and loud outburst that followed, I poured my heart out to him. Explaining why I hadn't told anyone about my leg and how I had cancer. I was full of stories of all I had been through. It was amazing how much pain I really was in. It's something about speaking your pain that makes it so much more real. What hurt me the most was the thought of how Candace could leave me on the cold sidewalk in front of the bar, helpless and she just walked away. She treated me like I was an animal. How could she leave me like that after all I had done for her? My confusion turned into anger and then to rage. Going on and on in a cycle until it dawned on me that I was there with Candace's boyfriend, and he was actually genuinely concerned about me. But why? Why was he listening to me? Why wasn't he concerned about his girlfriend? He was even giving me advice. It didn't make sense that a caring person like himself could even be interested in a woman like her. Well, to each its own.

Nico being there seeing the event unfold really made him see Candace in a different light because on a few occasions in the conversations, he would say, I can't believe she treated you like that. He would say she's dumb ass wrong.

I couldn't resist the urge to ask him why he was there in the first place. He said it was because he knew we had plans to be there that night. He was coming to see if there was any truth to the rumors, he had been hearing that she had been sleeping with other guys and taking money from them. Even though I knew the truth to what he was speaking on, I just couldn't betray her like that. I took our sisterly bond too seriously. I believed in loyalty, even if she didn't. Nico and I spoke for hours of our problems and life in general. He was easy to talk to and Lord knows I needed that right now. Talking seemed very therapeutic to me. Our talk turned into a sharing of our dreams and aspirations, long term career goals, even our plans on leaving Baltimore to start over in other cities. I was actually impressed by Nico's conversation. He was well spoken and if Candace had never told me otherwise, I would have put money on him having attended college. Before long I noticed that it was now almost 5:00 AM in the morning and my cell phone battery had died. Desmond was going to be furious with me. It was definitely time for me to go before he called the police or something. This was far from my normal routine. I wouldn't be surprised if he was putting an APB out on me as we speak. I asked Nico to take me back to my car so I could drive home. Then he reminded me that the car was parked at the bar and it would be in my best interest to put back on my prosthesis. We were so engrossed in our conversation, that I didn't even remember that I was sitting there without my leg on. I got shy and embarrassed all over again. The process of placing the prosthesis on made me feel sorry for myself and I had a moment of weakness and began to scream at Nico. Why? Why me?

Why did I have to have cancer? Why was I the one that had to lose my leg? Why, God, why me? By now trying to help me Nico moved closer and grabbed my face, looked me in the eye and told me I was beautiful. He said to me that my beauty was all that a person would see if they were really here for me.

"Your spirit makes your glow indescribable. It would be an honor to be in your midst, and don't let anyone tell you differently. You have something special that you don't find every day in people."

Those words made me feel as if Nico knew me. I had only met

him one time before at Candace's house, but the way he spoke of me, you would have thought he had known me for years. "Thank you for saying that, Nico."

"Don't thank me, Alexis."

Believe me! For the first time I noticed that Nico had sex appeal. He was charming, so I could see what Candy saw in him. For a moment, the truck became quiet. I could hear my heart beating through my chest. I felt like something was about to happen, but how was I going to get out of this car before I did something I would regret? Before finishing my thought, Nico was kissing me. This had to be a dream, because these many bad things could not happen to one person in one night. Nico's hands began to explore my body and I knew I needed to stop it, but I couldn't get up the strength to stop. All the fight was gone so I relaxed my body and allowed myself to enjoy this man. I was committing adultery, so I knew it was the beginning of my demise. I was doing everything that I was against my whole life's principles and morals which embodied my character. How could I succumb to everything I hated? I truly realized at that exact moment that the flesh was indeed weak. I WAS WEAK!

Chapter 7

Candace (Bye Bitch!)

Zooming past a Maryland State trooper, I didn't even care if he pulled me over. I was in Alexis's car. Who did she think? She embarrassed me like that. I couldn't believe what had just happened. One leg? This ***** had one leg and was trying to play me like a fool. How in the world did I not realize that was what was wrong with her anyway? I just kept thinking of how stupid I had looked holding her up while her wooden leg fell on the sidewalk. I already knew I would be the laughingstock of my neighborhood. Baltimore was too small for this not to get around, and my reputation was done. Not to mention how many phones were out. I know we are going to be all over social media. I had a pretty good rep if you ask me. I was respected, well known, I look good, and men love me. The woman envied me. What more was there?

Money wasn't a problem because I could always get some dummy to pay my bills. Not to mention Nico wasn't a slouch. People loved him. He was the hottest promoter around and I was his woman. To think of all that being in jeopardy because of this ***** Alexis and her stupid leg was crazy to me. I was angry at myself for not catching on to her condition earlier. It made sense though. Now I understood why she would never wear heels and she was always going to some crazy specialist doctor way out in Linthicum, MD. I knew her perfect life was full of shit. Keisha kept telling me that, but damn, Alexis always came off to be so put together, never having a single hair out of place. She had the car, the house, the kids, and the husband. She even had the looks. Or so I thought. I had to laugh to myself when I thought of what Keisha would say. Who, by the way,

I would need to call before she heard about this incident from someone else. Plus, she would be the only one who would understand why I had left Alexis crying one legged ass laying on the floor at the bar. I know we will sit around laughing and joking about the evening all night. But before that I would need to let off some steam and that was the perfect job for Top. Top was my little plaything. We merely had sex with each other with no strings attached. I didn't get money from him though, and he didn't get oral sex from me. He was my feel-good man. He was the only one that knew what I liked, just the way I liked it. I never left him unsatisfied, and he definitely took care of me. We had an unspoken understanding, even if we saw each other while we were out on the town. Nobody would even know that we knew each other. He was a thug, a DMX type thug dude that I enjoyed having sex with from time to time.

I had made arrangements to meet up with Top on the east side of town at his cousin's house. For some reason I couldn't get my drunken ass over there fast enough. Being intoxicated always made for better sex between us. Before pulling onto the street where his cousin lived, I made sure my hair and makeup was in order. I wanted to look irresistible to him so we could have a great evening. I could see his tall brown skin from the time I turned the corner. He was 69. So it was hard for anyone to miss him, I got baited in by his eyes and sexy body. The way he towered over me was a turn on. First time I saw him it was at a basketball court, so his height didn't move me, but we did catch eyes. He has a great fashion sense which made him the most stylish man I knew. He stood out even on the basketball court. I had to have him. The only thing I could not stand about Top was his age. He was only 19 and acted every bit of it. We can never talk about anything past rap, music, and video games. I know I'm not the smartest girl in the bunch, but I was 31 so I needed to speak to someone who could relate to me a little bit. But sex? It was the universal language and he spoke mine oh so well. So my thought was FUCK it. I just concluded that I was okay with him being my boy toy and his old head chic. Upon pulling to park and parking I could see from the looks of the crowd around him that Top was in the company of some admirers. Rather than get into a senseless fight with some knuckle head teenage girl I would just summons him over to the truck without getting out. Seeing his reluctance made me remember that I was in Alexis 's truck and not my normal car. To make my identity more assuring I rolled down the limo tinted windows so he could better see me. Still a little hesitant Top walked over to the truck and planted a kiss on my forehead. The smell of marijuana smoke and liquor lingered outside the truck which made me more excited to get inside his cousin's house. After jumping into the passenger side seat, we went on a short ride to the end of the block and went into his cousin, Row's home. Once inside Top directed me to the room and I plodded down on the day bed. Instantly, I took off my shoes and jeans. I was ready, but the feeling wasn't the same since Tap grabbed the controller to the Xbox game and continued the NBA Live game, he had been previously playing. Annoyed by the whole scene, I pulled out my phone and began tweeting about the evening. Noticing the progression of anger in my face must have got to him, because next thing I knew Top was exploring the walls of my vagina with his tongue. Instantly I knew Top had to have been drunker than normal, since I had never been given this kind of treatment by him. Feeling a little tense, I began to clear my mind, only allowing myself to take in his next to a perfect technique. I was impressed as the feeling began to run deep in my body I became limp and pure pleasure became to pour from within me. Just as I began to think that this young man couldn't feel any better suddenly, I felt a foreign object being pulled from my lips, just enough to make my eyes pop open. The suspension was overwhelming, I jumped up and faced an outraged Top. He was horrified at what he had just extracted from my pussy with his teeth. Spitting and damn near vomiting while blurting out every curse word known to man. It was a condom! The one that must have been used by House earlier that day. I was at a total lost for words so, doing the only thing I could do, I began to put on my clothes. The

61

vibration in the room was not feeling right and judging from the look on Top's face told the story. Since I had no desire to be on the cover of tomorrow's newspaper, I picked up the pace on my dressing never taking my eyes off of him. I apologized and assured Top that I did not know that condom was there. Growing more and more scared by his silence I opted not to get fully dressed and leave while I still had a chance. It would be in my best interest to get out of here. NOW! Without even thinking, I navigated my way out of Top's cousin's house. This situation was a mess, and my heartfelt apology did not diffuse it. I was thankful to be wearing boy shorts and my bra was all I had on when running into an accident outside his house. I had run out just in time because entering the truck and reversing it down the one-way street I was thinking to myself I wished I had listened to Nico and his endless pushes for me to back into parking spaces properly to avoid moments like this.

I could see Top holding a gun pointed directly at the truck and pulling the trigger. I was relieved that I had turned the corner before any of the bullets could strike the truck. Wow, that was close. Happy that finally the coast was clear, I was now shaking feeling like I was about to vomit, I pulled the truck over and put the rest of my clothes on and rolled the windows down. Tonight, had now proven to be the worst night of my life. It was like something from out of a movie starring me. I needed to call Keisha because I know not even she could top this one. Keisha had been through her own share of bullshit drama, but nothing on the scale of what all had just happened to me today. To me, Keisha was just misunderstood. She had a hard life, so she just always stayed in survival mode, which was not really all that bad. A victim of circumstances is what I like to call her, and it wasn't my place to judge her. She was cool to me, my friend, and the only one I seem to have at this point. Just as I picked the phone up to call her, my mind ran on the bar parking lot and Alexis's face looking at me like a scared puppy. I don't know why other people's misery was so amusing to me. There were so many people staring at her, but I could have sworn I saw Nico looking at me when I looked into the crowd. I think I was just seeing things since he was supposed to be in Washington DC. I hope it wasn't him. I would hate for him to witness me abandoning one of my closest friends like that. I couldn't have him thinking that bad of me, shit in his eyes. I'm perfect. He might believe the worst of me and leave me or something. At the end of the day, he is all I really need. I'm just fucking around with all these other dudes for fun. Men do this all the time. Why can't us ladies have some fun too?

Chapter 8

Keisha (I told you so!)

Just hang up the phone from Candace I had heard all about the crazy evening out with Alexis. I was surprised at what happened but didn't put it past her. I never trusted her or liked her for that matter. It was no wonder that her cripple ass would try to use some girls like us for people to accept her on the social scene. I felt a sense of happiness, that miss thing was outed. I hope she was somewhere crying her eyes out. Honestly though, I needed to direct my attention elsewhere because I was still trying to figure out why I hadn't received a call from Nico last night. It wasn't like him not to call or follow through with our appointments. I had called both of his phones, I know, over fifteen times between last night and this morning. Maybe he fell asleep or something. Either way, I needed to know why he would feel it was okay to stand me up. Nico wasn't my man, I know, but I still felt a degree of possessiveness over him. Even if we were not exclusive, I still wanted him to give me attention as if I was his one and only and up until this point he always did. So why was this night any different? I needed some answers from him, and I wanted them now. I was so angry. I even went as far as to tell Candace I had been stood up by my boyfriend in our earlier conversation in an effort to try and make myself feel a little better. She was just as shocked as I was being as though I never gave her highlights on our relationship. It gave me a rush to share facts about my fling with her, man, without her even knowing. Just speaking of Nico and my relationship made me have an orgasm on the inside... The only way that I would be able to get any details about where Nico would be was to call and question Candace herself, which would be risky, but it was exactly my style. ("Stupid ass" thinking to myself why didn't I just question her while I had her on the phone a second ago. Now it's going to sound crazy if I call her back now asking questions.) I found that being secretive always raised suspension but placing things right in front of people's faces always seemed to throw them off. Directing someone's attention elsewhere made it easier for a person like me. So, I called her and simply asked her, did Nico come home last night? She didn't hesitate at all to tell me he hadn't returned home yet, adding that she had been calling him and he hadn't been responding to her calls. She never even questioned why I was asking her all these questions prompted me to continue grilling her. She didn't reveal anything to me that I didn't already know. She did, however, say something about thinking that she had seen him outside the bar last night but wasn't sure. This girl had to be really stupid since there was no way I would think that I saw my man somewhere and not investigate. But not everyone was like me. This goes to show why I was fucking her man and she wasn't.

Now, with all the information I needed, I hung up the phone on Candace saying, "BYE GIRL!" And hanging up. Where could he be? I racked my mind for hours before he finally called.

"Where the hell have you been?"

"My bad. I had something important to take care of and lost track of time."

"Well, I don't like being stood up. And besides, what could be more important than spending time with me?"

"What? Girl, get your mind right. You are my side Bitch and that's all you are. Don't lose your mind and forget your place."

His words left me completely speechless on the other end of the phone, which didn't happen very often. I prided myself to be a woman of many words and quick with the comeback. I was sure to always get the last word and have the upper hand in the word fight. But this time my mouth remained open as he followed with how it had been nice while it lasted, but he was done. Not believing what I had heard, I fired back. "You're crazy. You're not going anywhere. I'm the best piece of *** you ever had. What are you feeling all sensitive about, your weak ass girlfriend? She will never be me. That's why you're with me every time you get a chance. I'm not worried. I know you'll be back." Somehow trying to convince myself that the words that were coming out of my mouth were true, but his tone really had me feeling he was definitely serious.

"Girl, you're delusional, Keisha. You were always just something to do. When all else failed, I would call you. Truth be told, your pussy is a bottomless pit, a black hole. Your ass is clueless of what it is that a real man, really needs. That's why no man stays with you long enough for you to pull up your panties. You're garbage. And as far as Candace, I already know she's a hoe. Shit the bitch hangs with you. My feelings aren't in it, baby. I was just getting my dick wet. I got a woman who leaves a nigga satisfied."

His words were harsh and cut deep. All I could do was hang up the phone with a vindictive, "Fuck YOU!"

I paced the floor back and forth, wondering what had just happened. Who was that? Nico would never speak to me like that. Better yet? What made him switch up on me? Or who? I didn't realize how much I had cared about Nico until right now. I felt as if I had lost my best friend or something. This **** was weird. My world felt like it was moving in slow motion. The thought of him not touching me again was unimaginable to me. My only focus now would be getting Nico back, making him see that I was the only one for him and he was the same for me. Vowing to myself to take down anyone who came between me and him and the love that I had just grown to realize I had for him that was including Kansas. Absent to give Nico time to cool down, I decided against calling him back until later, making up my mind that if Nico did not answer my call or wasn't receptive to my contacting him later, I would need to resort to more drastic measures. This may even mean going into his workplace or even places that I thought he would be. I was ready to make a scene if need be. If anything, Nico hated more was being in the middle of a drama scene. He hated drama. I was willing to do whatever it took to make him listen to me. The mystery still remained where all this was coming from, and who exactly was this woman who made him change up on me? And I knew it had to be a woman. What else would make a man act out of character? By now I was really fired up and in no mood to be bothered. When Tyrone came downstairs complaining about the fitted hat I had just bought him, I lashed out at him, telling him to take the shit back if he didn't want it. I didn't care... Not taking my words too kindly, Tyrone grabbed me by my neck and threw me to the floor punching me in the face. It happened so fast I hadn't even realized I had lost consciousness. It's sad to say, but this isn't unusual to me, since this is his way of showing his love for me. I believe every female should get a good ass whooping from their man every now and then. If he doesn't, he doesn't give a damn about her in my eyes.

Chapter 9

Alexis (The Storm)

Awakening to a loud blast of thunder, I lay in my bed submerged beneath the blanket, leaving only enough room for me to gaze out of the window. Hurricane Earl forecasters had been anticipating hitting Maryland all week, had finally showed its face. This made no difference to me anyway because I had already decided that I would never show my face outside the doors of my house again. I was still so confused about my traumatic experience, a lot of which was now a blur to me. I think it was just my brain's way of sparing me from all the gloomy details. With a hell of a hangover, I couldn't even remember how I got home. The last thing I remember was closing my eyes and freeing my mind over all my problems, then making the horrible mistake of sleeping with Nico. Truly, I now understood how people could commit the unthinkable act of adultery while under distress. It was just like I wanted to be out of pain, so bad I would do anything to make it go away. I would have never had sex with him under any other circumstances, I was sure about that. I was so angry at myself for losing control, allowing this indiscretion to happen. Now I was in jeopardy of losing my marriage too. My mind raced back and forth between Desmond and what happened and what could happen if he ever found out? My life and my kids' life would change forever and I was the cause of it all. If only I had been honest. One secret was going to cost me everything. I began feeling more like a villain instead of the victim.

I was still left with the task of telling Desmond what happened. He was bound to find out, but I could never picture myself telling him about Nico. I needed to think of a story of where I had been last night before he came to his own conclusion. Desmond hadn't been in the room since I had been up, but I knew he was soon to show his face. Laying around for another hour, I decided to pick myself up and go take a bath to regain my composure. Staying depressed wasn't my style anyway. I prided myself on how I managed to always take control of situations. Once I stepped into the bathtub, I slipped my leg off and laid it next to the bathtub. The bubbles in the water surrounded my naked body once I reclined back into the tub. Feeling completely relaxed, I closed my eyes. I began dreaming of a cold daiquiri and walks on a sandy white beach with the one I love. This confused me. Since my feelings were in a weird place. Yet and still my dreams felt so real. I could almost feel the heat from the sun on my skin. If only I had the ability to make my dreams reality. Snapping back to reality I began to think of how bad things had become in a matter of hours. I had managed to turn my life upside down. I just couldn't shake the feeling that things were going to get worse before they got better. But right now, I just needed to appreciate the quiet before the storm sinking further into the water while listening to the raindrops hitting the window started putting me into a trance. It was like it rocked me to sleep as if I were a baby. I had only been asleep for what felt like a minute when I heard "Lex. Lex."

"Alexis."

"WHAT?"

I hate it for someone to wake me up when I was sleep. Even if I was in the tub. It was Desmond trying to get me up and out of the now cold bath water. Noticing all the bubble bath being gone made me realize that I had been asleep way longer than I originally thought. As I sat up to retrieve my towel, he picked me up, carrying me all the way to the bed, wrapping me up in a clean, warm towel he had already laid out for me. How couldn't I love this man? He always looked out for me and made sure I was good.

Taking A good look at Desmond he didn't seem the same. He almost looked as if he aged over the last few hours. His face looked tired, like he had been up for days. We both could feel the elephant in the room. It was time to speak about last night, so I just jumped in feet first, opening the conversation with Desmond. "I'm sorry about last night. Babe, things got out of hand and I was really drunk. Following with I've got sick and then..."

I couldn't say the words. They just would not come out of my mouth. Pausing for a moment and still nothing. He was waiting for me to finish, annoyed him., He wanted to slap my face. I could see it. At this point, I'm not so sure I would blame him if he did. Not uttering another word to Desmond, I just turned away and left the room. This wasn't all that bad since I really was not prepared to answer questions about the evening. I had said all that I was prepared to say hopefully. Sorry was enough for him. I put my clothes on and went down the stairs to see where he had disappeared to. After searching the house, I went to the basement or the lions den as he likes to call it to find Desmond playing on his self-made Baltimore Ravens Pool table. Damn. Why was approaching Desmond so hard for me?

Answering my own question. I just knew how much he expected from me. He held me to the highest regard, and I never wanted to disappoint him. I just could not measure up to what he wanted me to be. I was supposed to be a devoted wife and super mother. How was I to explain that all I was is a drunken, adulterine Bitch. But here goes nothing, with one last look up to the sky, asking God to give me strength, I just began to tell him from A-Z what happened. However, omitting the piece of me sleeping with Nico. The uncomfortable details of the event became too much for Desmond, so he just asked me to stop. My husband tends to take my problems and pain as if they were his own. I got blessed with a man that really loved me for me. After a short pause in the conversation, Desmond asked me to repeat the story slowly. And one more time so he had it clear. We briefly spoke of the subject again and it was over.

According to him, he knew the true story. I could see it bothered him a lot though since he offered to me of calling his little cousins to handle Candace. Those little girls made fighting a sport. They took it as a s e n s e of fun. It was a way to keep them in shape, like a workout. However, in my eyes it was done. I was getting over it, and her. Candace had won this battle, but not the war. It was better this way. Plus, my absence was going to bother her. She was gonna miss me. I knew that for sure. Plus, God will take care of her, and I really believe that to be the truth. So, I wash my hands of the situation and let it slip off my back. I could almost feel in that instant, the real me coming back. My faith in God always gave me comfort. I consider myself spiritual, but I wouldn't say I was religious. Lord, but after yesterday all I could say is I was certainly definitely a sinner.

Chapter 10

Candace (Nico!)

It was Friday night, and I was glad because I knew that the parties and the alcohol would be endless. Lord knows I needed a drink. After all I had an awful week. I had made plans with Keisha, and we were definitely hitting the town tonight. I started early, pouring myself a shot into my solo cup. My day had been going alright, if you ask me being outside with the neighbors all day had done me a lot of good. I got all the tea on who got locked up and who was fucking who on my block. We sat around reminiscing on old times, even sharing a laugh about Alexis and her leg. It had gotten around town. It started becoming more and more amusing to me as the days went by, but I was done with it. I knew I had been a jerk to her but that was okay with me. Right now, I just needed to focus on Nico and him taking care of home. His absence had been weighing heavily on my mind. Ever since that night he had been acting distant from me. I was unclear why, prompting me to put in some extra quality time with him. Just in case it was me, I needed to give him a little special attention. Something had to be wrong since he had been quiet and uninterested in sex, which never had been a problem with us. We may have fought in all the other rooms in the apartment, but the bedroom was our oasis, a place where we made music for real. The drastic change made me very uneasy, and his passes were aggressive. His attitude didn't help. Tapping into his emotions was a gift of mine. See, Nico had said, nobody was ever emotionally tuned into him like I was. This made our bond unbreakable.

Keisha had called me earlier and questioned me on Nico's whereabouts? And where I thought he could be, which had been strange to me, but I wasn't too worried since I was almost positive that she was not his type of chick. She was just a nosy bitch! No, forget that. I am positive she wasn't his type. He was a man with standards. Plus, she was more worldly than me, so that made her definitely out of the running. I had always known he was not a fan of women that were in the streets. Really, I was surprised that he was even with me. But shit for real, I have class... I mean I even eat sushi. I be on my Cosby Show shit!!! I keep cranberry juice in my house. Nico didn't know any other females that did that.

I knew just how to reach Nico though, seeing as though he never went an hour without checking his Facebook page. He used that social media network for just that, to be social with everybody. As well as keeping up on the latest hot spots around the area he kept up on who was trending, and exactly what the people wanted. I was positive by leaving him a message in his inbox would trigger his attention. I knew he stayed with me. I held the upper hand. This was my Section 8 voucher, that got me this place, but he paid all the bills. Still in all, I demanded respect from him. If I even reference to the fact that I thought something was disrespectful to Nico he would reconsider doing it. He was a respectful person like that. He believed in giving people the respect they deserved. So, with this in mind, I opted to make sure to make mention of the blatant disrespect that he had been displaying by not coming home last night. After writing the message to him, I waited for hours for a response with no prevail. He did not respond. This cut through me like a knife. Things didn't feel right. Something was very wrong. In the next hours I went over, and over our relationship in my head. Examining exactly how I felt about him and where I would want our relationship to go, coming up with the same sad resolution every time. I was a Bitch to him and he had all the rights in the world to leave me, but not without a fight. After all, Nico was my man and nobody else's. If I was being truthful to myself, he was the best man I had ever dealt with. But fuck all of that, I needed to get ready. Keisha was gonna be here any minute now.

Waving goodbye to Keisha at the end of a long night of partying. She had invited me out and I felt it would be a great way to get my mind off of Nico and how I hadn't heard from him in almost 24 hours. It was around 2:30 AM and I was ready for bed. I turned to put the lights on in the house. When I saw a shadow that resembled a figure sitting in my dining room chair causing me to scream out to the suspicious figure in my house.

"Who is that?"

He spoke back to me in a calm tone, saying to me. "You're a heartless hoe."

"Nico? What the hell are you talking about and why are you sitting in here in the dark? You scared me to death." I turned the lights on just to give me the added reassurance that it was indeed Nico that I was talking to. Once I could see Nico I could see how angry he was. I knew he had heard what happened to Alexis. Laughing under my breath, I said, "Oh, you did!"

"What was that all about?" He asked.

It was kind of feeling like he had taken the incident personally, but I did not jump the gun and decided to feel him out.

"I thought she was your girl, Candace?"

"My girl? Nico, please. What the hell do I look like hanging out with a bitch with one leg? That hoe is a cripple. What the fuck? Do I look desperate for friends? What can she do for me but slow me down? I mean, I guess she's cool, but I'm not in the business of keeping no cripples."

I could see the look of disgust on his face instantly, but it didn't matter to me much. How did he find out about what happened anyway? Turning my focus back on him, I asked him, "Why are

74

you so concerned about her anyway? She's a nobody. She's nothing. She is wasting space if you ask me. I just don't understand why she would even want to live her life like that. If that was me, I would have slashed my throat. Man, who is really going to love that girl for real besides her Mama. This really makes me wonder why Desmond is even with her. He must have an insurance policy on her or something."

After rambling a few looking up at him I could now notice that Nico was in a state of severe rage. "The way I see it is you're the nobody, Candace. You aren't shit and everybody knows it but you. See the Word on the street is you treat your friends worse than you treat your enemies. Your reputation is done. While they were looking and laughing you were being recorded and being talked about. No matter how you look at it, no one wants a person like you as a friend. What type of grown woman worries about what people think, anyhow? You care more about these streets than you do your kids. That's why your daughter has little to no respect for you. I'm done with you! I'll be out of your house today. And after I leave, I want you to never call me again. And by the way, your so-called best friend Keisha isn't shit either. While you were worried about following behind her every minute, she was worried about trying to fuck your man every time you turned your back. But you should know that already since all you hoes think alike. By the way, just so that you know Shorty dick game is better than yours by far."

Time felt like it stopped at that very moment. Did he really just tell me that about the one person I called my friend? She was the only woman I trusted. Just to be clear that I heard Nico correctly, I asked him to repeat himself. "What did you say?"

"I've been fucking Keisha behind your back for months. We saw each other out at one of the parties I was promoting, and I slept with her that night in my truck. You know the truck she told you was so nice and great to have a quickie in. Yeah, it was, because she had already done it. She couldn't get enough of your boy. She has been coming back ever since."

Nico had no remorse for what he had done. It was almost as if he was getting pleasure out of telling me this. It made no sense to me since I had not done anything to him for him to seek this type of revenge. I couldn't imagine in a million years Nico would treat me like this. He was usually such a laid-back person. I could handle the part of him cheating on me. What I couldn't handle was with whom he cheated on me with. Keisha was like my family. We were sisters. She had broken every code in the book. So much was racing through my head. I had mixed emotions about everything. I wanted to rip Nico's dick off, but not as bad as I wanted to put a bullet straight through Keisha 's chest. It was a good thing that I feared prison more than I feared taking her life. Because if there was any way I could make her disappear without going to jail, I would do it. For some reason, the feeling of betrayal by her was greater than by him. The sad truth was, I expected it from Nico. After all, he is a man.

By now, Nico had begun to take his bags to his truck. Watching him from the living room couch, all I felt was hatred towards him. In my mind, I had always planned out what I would do in an event like this one. However, for some reason I was doing the complete opposite. I was numb. There weren't words to describe the level of hurt and betrayal I felt. But there was one thing for sure I would get even with Keisha if it was the last thing I did. She wouldn't even know it was coming. Since I had no plans on calling Keisha at this point to confront her. Traveling upstairs to my room, I settled in front of one of the four windows that faced the front of the house, allowing me to see Nico loading the last bit of his belongings into his truck. The full reality of what had just happened overwhelmed me as the tears began to fall, my stomach grew sicker and sicker. I had just lost my man, my best friend, and the only true friend I had. I treated her like dirt, and now she was gone too. All in 48 hours. What could happen next? Me being who I am, I could never let things go this easy. Keisha would have to pay for this. She had Ruined my whole life, and I was determined to take hers from her. If not physically, it would be mentally. She was going to pay one way or the other, since the best way to fight your enemies is to join them. That's exactly what I would do. I opted not to let Keisha know what I knew about her and Nico. She would have to find out the hard way, my way. My get back would definitely be better than my setback.

Chapter 11

Keisha

I needed to relax. I was stressed and the only thing that could cure this problem would be a little retail therapy. Seeing as though I had a black eye, I would need to wear a hat and my new Versace shades on my journey off to the nearest mall. I could always find money to go s h o p p i n g . Shopping was one of the only things I had in common with Alexis. Moving through the mall at a peaceful pace made a great day of shopping and drama free fun. Paying close attention to the stores that had sale signs in the store window in hopes that I could catch a glimpse of something I could afford. I began to reminisce on the times I had with Tyrone and how he would take me on shopping sprees just to put a smile on my face. These days, it felt like he would rather put bruises on me instead. Moving about in the mall, I was bound to see somebody I knew. The thought never crossed my mind that I may see somebody that I didn't want to see as well. It was quite a shock to me when I saw Alexis. She was surprisingly beautiful. Her hair and nails were done as usual. For some reason I had pictured her being all stressed out since the incident. Maybe even balled up crying somewhere, but she didn't appear that way at all. She was with her kids and a lady who mirrored her as if they were twins. So, I assumed it was her sister, as much a s I would have loved not to speak pretending that I had not even seen her, we had already caught eyes and were headed straight towards each other. I readjusted my glasses and hat to ensure she would not see my eye or hair. They were both in a bad state. I always make sure my clothes were put together nicely so the attention would be on them rather than on me. Usually I craved attention, but my black eye made the attention unwanted.

"Hey girls, how are you?" Embracing Alexis, I couldn't help but comment on her perfume, since it caught my attention before I even drew near to her. The smell was intriguing. I was completely captured by it. So much so that it would be the topic of our conversation the whole three minutes that we spoke. I made sure to acknowledge the fact that I heard she had a hard time a few days back at the bar. I even offered my apologies for Candace's behavior. The references to the incident made Alexis, as well as her sister, visibly uncomfortable. They quickly changed the subject and said their goodbyes and were off. I was satisfied!!! I succeeded in making her feel like shit. Having mastered being a phony fair-weather friend had worked again. I hated Alexis and she was too naive to see it. What a retard. It must have been hard, being both retarded and crippled, I thought to myself. I had to laugh while watching her walk away. I didn't know how we didn't notice sooner about her wooden leg. Her walk was quite weird if you ask me. Not wasting any more time, I continued on my shopping journey once again strolling around the mall. Retail therapy didn't seem to help as much as I thought it would have, I was still depressed.

Now smoking a blunt was surely going to finish off the job of making me feel more like myself. I felt the need to visit my old neighborhood to get some good quality weed. This bullshit weed was giving me a headache. I knew just who I needed to go see to get that fire. I started my journey over to my old hood. I learned everything I knew from that neighborhood. I wouldn't have any survival skills if it wasn't for the streets over there. It was like the people around the block where I grew up, live by a different creed than most others. I was a grimy gutter like bitch, and I knew this. But my friends from that neighborhood, my old neighborhood, were way worse than me. Thinking about this made me realize that this would be a perfect place for me to go get some ideas on how to get Nico back and get rid of Candace altogether. I was willing to do anything but kill somebody to get her back. So, the options were endless. Plus, I would need to deal with whoever this girl was that has Nico's nose wide open. I wasn't willing to share him with no one else. If he was going to leave Candace, it was going to be for me and not anybody else.

Finally, I made it to my grandparents block just in time to see the police roping off a crime scene with the yellow caution tape. This was a all so familiar scene just made me shake my head. There was always something going on down here. The presence of police was a regular ordeal around these blocks. Still with the police present, the crime seemed to never decline. It was as if the police presence made the criminals more active. The guys around here love doing shit right under the cops' noses. It was a game for them. A few years back, the mayor put in blue light cameras all throughout the city. The cameras were placed on the light poles and could catch every angle on streets in the city where there was an increase in crime. These cameras just gave the crime seeking people star power since they were now on film committing the act. The local news channels would play clips of the films asking for help in capturing everyone involved in the crime. This only made the people involved famous in the hoods since we had a strict no snitching policy. Turned off by the whole scene, I opted out of watching any more of what was going on? Pushing past the crowd, I started my journey down to my grandmother's house, which was about. Six houses down the street. I could see her and about half a dozen people on her front porch. All of their attention was focused down the block at the commotion. Making it easier to sneak up on them.

"SCREAMING!! What the hell y'all Looking at?"

Scared out her mind, my grandmother nearly dropped the cigarette out of her mouth. My cousin went straight for his gun that was on his hip. After realizing it was me, we all began to laugh after they warned me never to do that again. We sat on the front porch for hours, sharing old stories from our younger days and listening to music. The word got around fast that I was visiting, so what started out to be a few people was now over fifteen people and my grandmother cooking out on the grill in the front yard. It wasn't exactly the best weather, but it was a party. Grandma Bee Bingo's friends came over and some of my boys from the block. This was just how things happened around here. I got a chance to speak to one of my friends about my Nico dilemma. She gave me some good tips, and even shared some of the tricks she played in the past on her last boyfriend. Around 11:30 PM, I decided to leave since this was the time things started to get crazy around here. Usually around this time everybody was drunk, and their fuses went off faster making the drama and altercations happen in seconds. Everyone tried their best to stay off the front just because bullets had no name on them. So, the party had relocated to the back alley. Shooting off their guns was the dope boys' hobby, especially these young guys. They were different. They really did not care about human life. They had no morals, and they had no code that they lived by. Things had definitely changed from when I was younger. I went inside to say my goodbyes to everyone when my grandmother stopped me. She reminded me that she loved me no matter what she heard about me. "Grandma Bee loves you, my baby." I felt the lump swell up in my throat. The tears were about to come, but I was fighting them off. Grandma Bee was the only one that could get me like this. I loved her so much. I stuttered.

As I said, I love you to my grandma back. She pulled me near and then kissed my face. I always admired this woman. She was my hero. Just as I began to turn away, she grabbed my face and slid the shades off my eyes. Then she asked me when was I going to start loving myself enough to know that I didn't deserve this black eye? She never seemed to amaze me. I was never able to get anything past her. My grandmother knew me better than I knew myself. I was at a loss for words. But a response wasn't what she wanted. She wanted to plant the seed in my head and allow it to grow. Grandma Bee was a wise woman, she always would say in order for a seed to grow, it had to be placed in the proper environment and allowed to mature at its own pace. She would say no matter how much you water a plant, it will still only grow when it is ready. The water and the soil you put the seed in only determines how strong the plant will be. And that's just what she did. Silently, I expressed my gratitude for her kind words with a simple head nod and embraced her. I left my grandmother's house that night feeling embarrassed and ashamed of myself for letting the woman that I admired and adored all my life see me in this kind of state. Growing up, she had been my rock ever since I could remember, I always wanted to emulate her. Which wasn't a bad thing, since all the other women in my life were either drug addicts or prostitutes or both. They were criminals, drug dealers, hustlers, boosters, the list goes on, but not Grandma Bee, she was the only constant making living up to her standards a must. It was amazing how she commanded everyone's respect. She didn't have to do much, just by the way she carried herself or the way she would look at you, you felt the need to give her the utmost respect. People in the street gave her respect without even saying anything. I loved her strength, and that's about the only thing that she passed down to me. There was just something about her seeing me like this that got to me. I think it made her feel like a failure because of my poor choices. How could I allow her to feel this way when I knew her upbringing was embedded deep within me? I just chose to go down the wrong path. It was easier to do so. It made it easier to accept my failures. There were no expectations when you know you're doing wrong. Once leaving my grandmother's house, I didn't feel down for long. Depression was a sign of weakness, and that was one thing I wasn't. I wasn't weak. So as soon as I hit my grandmother's front door, I was over it. All I could do was think about how I would put my plans to get Nico back in effect.

First thing was first, I needed to get rid of Tyrone. This will be easy, seeing as though Tyrone had a little problem that he thought I wasn't aware of. I guess somewhere along the lines he felt as if it was okay to touch little girls. My oldest daughter had come to me after he had moved in with us, which was about two months after we met. She told me that Tyrone had come into her room and made her touch his penis. He helped her stroke his penis until he came. She also said he made her take her clothes off and dance for him Sometimes grinding on him while she was sitting on his lap. I asked her when it happened, and she said it started like the second day he moved in, I never confronted him. I was just too in love to let something like that get in the way of my happiness. I mean, he hadn't penetrated her (at least I think) he hadn't, and he was doing what some young boy was going to ask her to do pretty soon anyway. Shit it was practice is how I looked at it. Not too long after she told me, I came home early from the club and saw him in her room, jerking off in front of her bed. She was naked and on the bed crying. There was Jodeci Come and talk to me playing loud in the background. Tyrone was sitting on one of my kitchen chairs that he had taken from my table and placed in front of my daughter's bed. I didn't let either one of them see me, but I knew she was telling the truth at that point. Turning around and tiptoeing back down the hall, I let him finish and pretended to have not seen anything, even pretending to be asleep when he entered the bedroom. Tyrone got into the bed and immediately started stripping down. Pushing his naked body up against mine. It felt like almost instantly we started having sex. It was intense! I couldn't help but think that my daughter's naked body was what Tyrone was imagining while penetrating me. I knew that one day this information would come in handy. I was actually glad that I hadn't said anything or reacted too hastily when my daughter gave me the information. I figure now that if I pretend to catch him and threaten to call the police if he didn't leave, I could get rid of him for good. I just needed to catch him in the act again. This shouldn't be a problem since Tyrone Would always make sure that my daughter was there when I would leave the house. However, since I depended on him to pay the rent, I will just tell him if he stops paying the rent, I will call his probation officer and get his ass locked up. He was on parole, and he was on his last strike with his parole officer. If he had any more problems with the law, he would send him back to prison to back up his fifteen more years left on his sentence. After that was taken care of, the real task would begin which was stealing Nico from Candace.

Chapter 12

Alexis ("I want my husband")

After leaving the mall, my sister and I still had some running around to do. I had a wonderful night planned out for Desmond and myself, I had already purchased the perfect outfit to wear. All I would need to work on now would be a great meal and a babysitter for the kids. The babysitting part shouldn't be that hard since Auntie Dana, my sister, always loved watching her nephews. If she didn't want to, I could remind her that she owed me a favor. So, on the ride home, I asked her, and she was more than happy to oblige. With that taken care of, it was time to figure out the meal we would have, I called Desmond 's favorite restaurant and placed an order for carry out. I was determined to remind him of how much a good wife I could be. I wanted him to remember why I was worth all the headaches that he had been having these past few weeks. Desmond was always down for a little role-playing, so I went down to the toy store and picked up a children's football goal. To go along with the football player Halloween costume, I had picked up from the mall earlier.

I bumped into Keisha while I was at the mall. Lord, forgive me, but the more and more I was around that woman, the more I come to grips with the fact that I hated her. I know it's wrong to hate, but babbbby, I hate that woman!!!! She just gets under my skin. I just can't say it enough. The girl is just all around trash. I couldn't help but feel sorry for her kids for having to deal with a woman like that on a day-to-day basis. I truly believed that she would sell out her first born if it benefited her. All I could do was pray for them. I prayed that they get away from her before she could do them any irreversible damage.

I felt like this seeing her walking through the mall looking all crazy with some thigh high boots on and in a blonde wig. She even had on some dark sunglasses with the wide lenses like she was some type of movie star. A floppy hat covered most of her face. Looking like a ghetto, Marilyn Monroe. She had the nerve to be looking my sister and I up and down as if we looked crazy. I mean, she was the one parading around the mall with a black eye. The dummy didn't check to see if her lenses were dark enough on those cheap knockoff Versace sunglasses. I could see straight through them. Maybe next time she will get some black tinted shades instead of brown which was completely see through.

Everything was finally done. All that was left to do was to make magic with Desmond. I needed this night to go perfectly, but from the looks of things it was not going to go that way. My sister had just called and informed me that she was not going to be able. to watch the boys after all. The dinner that I ordered was getting cold, and in my attempts to keep it hot, I had just burned most of it in the oven. It seemed like my evening was going to turn out to be a disaster. In hopes to salvage the rest of the night, I ordered the kids to stay in the basement for the rest of the evening, which I knew wouldn't gonna go over well since they were used to having the full run of the house. Besides, how was I going to get down and dirty with my husband with fear of the kids popping in every minute? SHIT, all my hard work was going out the window right along with my enthusiasm about the night!

Just when I thought things couldn't get any worse, my cell phone rang. I could not believe that this BITCH had the audacity to ring my phone after how she had treated me. Her self-centered ass didn't even give me a chance to forget about the incident before ringing my phone, which was typical of Candace. The sun and the moon had to shine on her ass at all times, forget about anyone else's feelings, and to add insult to injury, she had just fucked up my whole evening. Now all I would be focused on was the nerve of her. There was no way I was going to be able to forget about this phone call in time to enjoy my husband. I had made up my mind that I would give her the best tongue lashing as soon as I picked up the phone. Swinging opened the phone, I promptly said to her, "You ungrateful Bitch. After all I've done for you. You treated me like some mud on your shoes, scraping me off on the sidewalk and keeping it moving. You are so lucky. I'm trying to get to heaven, because if I wasn't, I would come over there and wrap a metal pole around your fucking neck."

The silence and occasional sniffles coming from the other end of the phone caught my attention, sending me into another rage. "Wow, Candace tears. Are you serious? You could do better than that. I guess now you want me to believe that you have a heart, huh, Miss Tin man?"

I guess the Wizard of Oz reference got to Candace. Alexis, I know you're mad at me and you have every right to be, but I am sorry. But I'm hurting too."

"You're hurting too? I don't care about you. What about depressed, humiliated, embarrassed and angry, the list goes on. You made me feel worthless out there and I would have never done that to you. You will never understand the pain I feel."

"Lex, I know you're right and I'm so sorry. Please forgive me."

After about an hour of apologizing and crying, I felt so sorry for Candace. Not even one minute after I told Candace that I forgave her, she filled me in on what had been going on with Keisha and herself. She told me how Nico had broken up with her and Keisha had been sleeping with him the whole time. It didn't come as a surprise to me, since I had been having bad vibes about Keisha from the beginning. I have warned Candace about that woman over and over again. Still, I hated to see her so upset in the back of my mind, also wondering if she ever found out about Nico and me, what would happen? Besides being confused on why Nico would ever touch Keisha of all people. I mean, Nico was hot. He could have any girl he wanted, why Keisha?

Being as it was, and everything was all done, my back was against the wall, I asked Candace to watch the boys for me. She was happy to help me out, since it was the least, she could do. So, my plans were back on once again, but I was not completely out of the woods yet. I had to figure out how to keep my babysitter's identity from Desmond. He would not be okay with the situation. I always had a way of making a bad situation worse. However, I was comfortable with Candace because she was a lot of things, but a child abuser was not something that she was. I was sure that my babies were in good hands. With my mind at ease, I could direct my full attention to my husband.

Candace had just left with the kids when Desmond walked through the door. The timing couldn't have been better. The look on his face when he walked in made all the troubles I went through worth it. At that very moment, I knew I had my husband all to myself and I was determined to get us back on track. Our marriage was going to last, I was going to make sure of it. Which I would soon find out was the easy part. Keeping him there would prove to be the challenge...

Chapter 13

Candace (Revenge)

Keisha had been running through my mind all day. I could not think of anything else. I was beginning to become obsessed with getting even with her. It was what I thought of the first thing in the morning and the last thing I thought of at night. Since every war had to have a chief and soldiers, making good with Alexis was to my benefit. I was positive that she would be willing to jump on board with me and get Keisha back. My friendship with Alexis was completely conditional, even if she did not know it. The more I dealt with Alexis, the more she came across as a useless, needy woman. I mean, what kind of woman leaves their children with the same person that left them on the sidewalk crying their eyes out? It's a good thing that I don't believe in mistreating kids, or she really would be in trouble. Wow, she was way too gullible for me. Time and time again, she's solidified why She could only be a pawn in my game. I need strong people around me. I didn't have time nor the patience for the damsel and distressed. I was doing Alexis, a favor anyway. Fraternizing with people like me was only going to bring her a world of pain in the long run. I'm really teaching her a lesson.

I got the kids some pizza and movies to get them out of my hair. Then I focused on the details of my plan to get even with Keisha, getting even was mildly put compared to what I planned on doing to her. I have never believed in fighting fairly, so any day I allowed her to keep her head above ground was a gift.

The more I searched my mental roller rolodex, little cliff notes would pop up into my head of things Keisha had told me about her personal life. I remembered her telling me how one of her baby's father sold drugs and laundered money through a corner store over on the west side. It was relevant information, since the fastest way to get to a person like Keisha would be to cut off their money supply. Her son's father was her only real means of money, since she had no education not even a G.E.D. the only other thing she did was sell pussy from time to time. Nobody really wanted her ass, now since the word around town was, she had been ran through by everybody. Following up on a couple little details I put in an anonymous call to the feds about a drug and handgun operation being run through her baby's father's store. The feds didn't waste any time putting a task force together and raiding the store. Two men were busted, including both of her kids' father. This was really going to hurt Keisha. Once all her money stopped from child support. Her welfare check could never support her flashy lifestyle. The kind of female she was, Keisha would most definitely hit the streets. She will prowl every nightclub and every hot spot looking for her next victim. That meant any baller male or female with money that could fund her wants was a target. The crazy thing about guys that have money and hung out in clubs they always wanted to see a nice-looking chick on their arm. Most of them had a weakness for pussy and they had the money to afford any woman they wanted, but it couldn't be just any woman, they had to be the woman they dreamed of having when they didn't have any money. You know, the ones that look like the woman in the music videos and the women with the beautiful faces, perfect bodies and booty that looks like it was hand sculpted by God? I had to give it to her, looks and body was the one thing God had blessed Keisha with. She definitely knew how to use it to her advantage.

Since I knew Keisha's next move would be to go to the club, I had already put into effect my next move. I called Big Tony one of the bouncers at our favorite club. He would always let us in for free and he was pretty cool. But one thing about Big Tony, he had a huge mouth he talked more than females. I just slipped the bug in his ear just in casual talk. I told him that Keisha had gonorrhea and she had tested positive for syphilis too. I actually told him she was waiting for her results for HIV. He was way too much of a female to not tell anybody. By the end of the night, I knew it was gonna be all over town. No matter how good looking you are, if a guy thinks you are giving away more than just a little sex, they will not deal with you. Unless, of course, they were given away a little more themselves. I did not even need anyone to believe it was true. All I needed was to plant the doubt into their head. It would be enough for no man to want to come near her.

Image was everything to a flashy social bee like Keisha. Now I was not about to leave Keisha in a nice cozy townhouse while all this was going on, so I figured I would call her landlord since I had his number and pretended to be Keisha 's probation officer asking about her living arrangements. He wouldn't be too happy about this since, per her lease, there was a full page designated to not allowing any persons with felonies, arrest, or probation on the property. It stated that if this had occurred, it would result in violating the terms of the lease which will result in voiding of the lease in its entirety effective immediately. I figured she would have to leave within the month After hearing from Mr. White, this landlord did not play any games with his tenants, and he did not have to. There was a laundry list of people waiting to get into one of his properties. I smiled about my plan; it was flawless. On top of not having any money, she wouldn't have a man or a roof to put over her head nor her kids. By the time she noticed what was happening to her, it would be too late. Her whole world would be crumbling, and she would have no way to regroup at which time she would be desperate for a friend, and that's when I can reveal to her that I was the cause of her sudden deterioration. She should have never f*** with me. In Keisha and my world, the only thing that mattered was getting the last laugh, and if everything went as planned, it was my laugh to have. To some people this may seem harsh, but not to me. It showed that I was a force not to be reckoned with. Oh. It was an eye for an eye.

Keisha had called three or four times that day making small talk. I knew the only reason for her calls was to feel me out and see if I knew anything of her and Nico, but time and time again I remained calm and undetectable, never letting on that I knew anything. I was enjoying watching her sweat. She was like a fish out of water, all jumpy and on the edge. The next few days will be self-suicide for her. And All I planned to do was sit back and watch herself destruct.

Chapter 14

Keisha

At this point calling Candace was getting me nowhere, I couldn't seem to break anything out of her. I needed to find out what was going on with Nico. He had said it was over before but not like this. The suspicion was killing me, but I was still motivated and determined to get Nico back. He was just too precious for me to let go without a fight. He was important to me, so I was ready for whatever I needed to do. I still needed to find a way to get Candace out of the picture for good. She was more work than she was worth. Considering that I had taught Candace everything she knew, I wasn't worried about her in the least bit. She was a small fry to me. Taking care of her would be easy. I was more concerned about getting in touch with Nico and getting him to see how devoted I was to him. My newfound love for this man was eating away at me. The stress of worrying about him was taking its toll on me. It had now been about two weeks and I was still no closer to Nico than the day he called here all upset. Desperate times call for desperate measures, it was time to now pay Candace a little visit and informed her of what her dear friend had been doing with her man. I planned on cluing her in on all the juicy details. I wanted her to hate the sight of Nico. This will make all our lives much easier. For added assurance, I made sure I took my 45 just in case she needed a little more persuasion. One way or the other, she was going to leave my man alone.

Chapter 15

Alexis (shit! What Now?)

A few months had past, and things could not have been better between Desmond and me. After everything had happened with Nico, he just could not stop calling me. He called a few weeks after the night at the bar and confessed to me that he had been attracted to me the whole time, but what was once an attraction was becoming obsessive. He was always calling and showing up at my work. I even seen him outside of my son's daycare center. He went as far as to follow me home one night and sleep underneath my window. I knew he had done this since he would tap on the glass on the window every so often to let me know he was still there. This went on the whole night. It was amazing Desmond didn't hear him. It was almost as if he was not concerned about Desmond at all. I did have one more fling with him, despite my better judgment. I thought that it would satisfy his curiosity and make it easier for him to leave me alone. I must admit it was also to satisfy my own curiosity, so that I knew for sure if Desmond was the man for me. I realized I was happy in my marriage for the first time in years and he was trying to mess everything up. It did not work, though Nico was worse than before. He wanted to be with me and was going to stop at nothing.

The fact that I was two months pregnant didn't help the situation either. The pressure of keeping the secret from Candace and Desmond was taking its toll on me. Since neither one of them still did not know that Nico and I had slept together. Every week that passed I grew sicker and sicker with guilt. Desmond was once again in love with me, and I was possibly pregnant with another man's baby. I was positive that the guilt would kill me if I had not gotten it out, but how was I going to tell the man that I was in love with that I betrayed him in this way not once, but twice? Every time I try to reveal the secret of what I had done, I would think of my children and how their whole world could come crashing down. I was supposed to be the responsible parent and provide a drama free environment for them. Instead, I would be the cause of their whole lives changing. Who was I kidding? I was no saint; I was only human. I had made a selfish mistake that could cost me everything. What was I going to do?

While standing in the line to pay for my parking at the hospital parking garage, I felt a presence behind me. I could feel the warmth of the person's breath on my neck. It was Nico, I was almost sure of it. It was one of the antics I had become accustomed to him pulling. Not turning around for him to know that I was aware of his presence, with my back to him, I simply spoke out loud asking, "What are you doing here?"

"Alexis, do you really think I would miss the appointment of my baby girl?"

"Why do you keep saying that? What makes you so sure that this is your baby and that it's a girl?"

"Because a man knows Lex. A man can feel when a baby is theirs and when it's not, and I know that she's mine. The real question is when are you going to tell Desmond that it isn't his? He has the right to know."

Nico's words cut like a knife. I knew he was right... I was just much too big of a coward to do what I knew I needed to do. I was just so angry with myself for being in this position. But I was also mad at Nico. Somehow, I believe that he was capitalizing on the situation, while my life went to hell. Nico and I argued all the way to my car and after making sure I was safe inside of my vehicle, he left, but not before he followed me to my appointment. He waited in the lobby while I saw the doctor and made sure to question me about every little detail. I was annoyed with him, but it was kind of nice having a guardian around. It was like he was a guardian angel around me, the only difference is that I could see him. Nico showed up at the most unusual times. It was like he always knew when I needed him. Actually, I became accustomed to him popping up.

Several long but short months later, I had a baby girl named Nyla. She was beautiful and most importantly, healthy. I have been under so much stress that Nyla's health became a big issue. She was a fighter and remained strong through it all. I was amazed by her grace. No one could tell me she had not been here before. She looked at me as if she knew me from someplace else. Desmond couldn't have been happier. He adored his baby girl, and she adored him. Watching them draw closer only made me grow weaker. I was an awful person for allowing things to go this far and I would need to fix it. I wanted to inform Nico of my decision to come clean about everything. But for some reason, after days drew near for Nyla to be born, Niko started to come around less and less. Though he was present in the waiting room of the maternity ward when baby Nyla was born, making sure to stay out of the view of Candace or Desmond. The only reason that I was aware that he had been in the waiting area was because he had given a note to my nurse to give to me after Nyla was born. I even believe he had seen the baby in the nursery after I had her. I couldn't imagine how though. Since there was so much security around the maternity ward. There was even a special code you had to put into the elevator to go up to the nursery. They gave us (the parents) matching identifying bracelets to the baby to be permitted to see her in the nursery.

After that day, Nico vanished. I wasn't that alarmed at first because there was a lot of traffic coming in and out of my house. Also, the days after delivering Nyla, I hadn't been traveling alone, Desmond was always with me. He was being extremely protective of his girls as he would say, not allowing us out of his sight. The man even took his maternity days from work.

However, four weeks was way too long for him, Nico would've most defiantly popped up by now. I began to worry about him and selfishly started to fear that I would be left here alone to deal with the harsh task of coming clean from all the betrayal on my own. My anxiety started to take over and just like that I was in panic mode. All sorts of thoughts began to flood my mind.

About six weeks later, after picking up Nyla and the boys from my mother's house. I saw this dark SUV following a few cars behind us. My stomach grew knots, the hairs on the back of my neck stood up. I knew it was him, I had so many questions I wanted him to answer. For some reason I was even feeling nervous to see him. Catching every red light for miles at each stand still, I would look in my rearview mirror hoping to get just a glimpse of his face but each time the light would change before I could see him. Twenty minutes later, and what felt like a hundred lights, finally I parked in front of my house. So nervous about what was going to take place I just jumped out to get the boys into the house, instructing them to wait for me inside and not to open the door for anyone. I hastily jumped back into the car and pulled off with Nyla in the back sound asleep in her car seat. I pulled into the nearest gas station and waited. Not quite sure what I was even waiting for. I wasn't even sure it was Nico in that SUV. Turning off the car and collecting my thoughts, I needed a moment to think. It wasn't long before a shadow appeared alongside my car. He opened up the back door as if he was already aware that Nyla was there. The emotions began to overwhelm me. I was so relieved Nico was okay and that he was here with his baby girl. I was not ready to face him yet so while sitting in the front driver's seat I placed my head back onto the headrest, closed my eyes and asked Nico where he had been for the last few months. Just to hear a weak voice respond back in almost a whisper saying that he was always with us. He said he just observed from a distance. Taken back by his muted tone and loud troubling breathing patterns, I opened my eyes and turned to the back of the car. Not at all surprised to see Nico holding baby Nyla and staring at her, seemly captured by her beauty. She was a gorgeous baby. What did surprise me was the sight of Nico's skeletal body. He looked fragile, unable to hold up his own body weight. He looked tired, aged even. Looking up from Nyla noticing me watching him, Nico locked eyes with mine and complimented me on how in creditably beautiful our daughter was. He said she had gotten it all from me. The words did not register, only the corpse like figure had my attention. I was so confused. He did not look like the man I knew eight months ago not even six months ago. I just could not wrap my mind around his size which was now small enough that he could probably occupy the same car seat the baby was in. For Nico not to see the puzzled dismay look on my face, I scrambled to turn the overhead lights off, that I had put on for him to get a good look at Nyla. Beginning to shake uncontrollably as if my body had a mind of its own, I couldn't even control my hands, so I slid them beneath my bottom and rest my forehead onto the steering wheel. It was like God was preparing me to brace myself for whatever I was going to hear. When I heard Nico say, "Lex I'm sick!"

I didn't have to hear the actual words to know what Nico was about to tell me. The car drew deafening with silence. The only thing keeping me from screaming out to the Lord was the soothing sounds of my baby girl sipping from the bottle her dad was now feeding her. Nico followed up by stating the fact that he found out three months before Nyla was born that he was HIV positive. The air seemed to get trapped in my throat making it nearly impossible for me to catch my breath so much, so I had to exit the car. Nico promptly followed assuring me that he was unaware of his status when we slept together. He repeatedly apologized. Not hearing any of his apologies, all I could do was vision my children at my funeral. Seeing how upset I was, on lookers began to direct their attention in the direction of my car. Troubled by the stares Nico convinced me to get back in the car. I was at a loss for words, Nico then handed me an envelope holding a large sum of money and a letter to Nyla and myself that he emphasized should be read only after his passing. He told me that the doctors had informed him that the disease had been caught way too late and there wasn't much they could do for him. The whole thing was becoming too much for me to handle. I needed a minute, just one minute to rewind my life and correct some of the mistakes that I had made. I wanted this man to have never been in that bar that evening in hopes that it would change his and my outcome, and where we found our lives today, my head was just about to burst when just like that Nico kissed my cheek and lightly pecked Nyla little hand and exited the car.

Climbing into the back seat next to my baby girl, I took her from her car seat and held her in my arms. Looking down at her precious little face made my heart sink, to think that her life would suffer for the mistakes I had made. I thought of how unfair I had been to her and now to leave her in the cruel world without any parents and no one to tell her they loved her. It was not a burden that she should have had to carry. I couldn't blame her if she grew up to hate me. I hated myself for what I had done to all our lives. So many thoughts filled my head even ones of ending the two of our lives right there in that car. I figured I would be able to be a mother to her in heaven, if not on earth, but then my mind ran on the other lives that would suffer from me taking my own life. At that moment I realized that it would be impossible for me to make this right. Only the Lord could see me through this one, but not even his mercy was I deserving of.

Chapter 16

Candace (Little Nyla)

Alexis's new baby Nyla made me want to change my way of life. Knowing that having a beautiful family and a husband of my own was within my reach, I would just need to change certain aspects of my life, to achieve it. She gave me a new outlook on things. It was something about holding a little newborn baby in your arms that did something to people. Married with children always sounded too much like a cliche to me up until this point. I am not saying that I was any better than Alexis, but if she could have a family, why couldn't I? I have kids, but we always did our own things. They went their own way, and I went mine even to my two youngest were with their fathers at their grandparents' house most of the time. We all never felt too much like a family. I can't even remember the last time it was that all of us were at the house together, all right in the house together for that matter. I mean, look at Alexis. She was handicap, a woman with medical problems who, despite everything, beat her battle with cancer and went on to have three beautiful kids and a husband who adored her. If she could after all of that, wake up in the morning and face the world with a smile on her face and never complain. Why should I being a healthy woman who had never been sick a day in her life? Think that I was not capable of having the same things. Happiness!!!! We all are in disservice, right? Alexis actually amazed me to see how strong she was to keep on going through life and picking herself up time after time again. Even when I betrayed her and proved to be unworthy of her friendship and or love, she went against what We called human nature and forgave me anyway. I was not too big on religion, but I did know what I was told about it by my aunts and uncles, even my mother. I knew enough to know that Alexis was no ordinary person. She had to be an angel sent to us by God to show us non-believers that He is real. I didn't know where all those things were coming from, but I was abnormally sensitive today... I felt like the weight of the world was on my back. I just needed to get out of this house. I rushed to retrieve my purse from my room and started out the door. I opened the front door, and started down the street to the bus stop, I was going to Alexis's house. I wanted to see her face to face and tell her how horrible I felt and sorry I was for being such an awful friend to her. Even though this had happened months ago, and we were good, now I just had to say it. I needed her to know how much of an inspiration she was to me.

I was stopped in my tracks to see a man sitting on my front stoop. I was not that concerned since people around here always sat on others front stoops. I turned my back to lock my door, "Candace, can I talk to you for a minute?"

I recognized the voice, but the face did not look familiar to me. As the stranger began to talk, I realized that this was no stranger, it was Nico sitting in front of me. His body was pale, and he seemed lifeless. I couldn't imagine what could have had him in such a poor health except drugs, but that was not Nico's style. He was too health conscious to engage in taking drugs. I was confused as I watched him talk. I kept feeling like I was stuck in a bad dream where my lifelong lover had died and came back to me to tell me all that he had not while he was living. It was as if Nico's spirit had died, and he was coming to me in his flesh alone. His poor state got to me badly. My experience working for Hospice, a note as a nursing aide gave me a little knowledge of what his signs of illness could be stemming from, but they all were much too bad for me to come to grips with. I decided against jumping to assumptions. But to rid him from the burden of having to tell me himself I said it for him, "Nico, do you have cancer?"

Only shaking his head Nico said, "No, I have AIDS."

Just like that, the truth was out. Nico was HIV positive. At no point, though, did I think of the fact that Nico was not only trying to inform me for him, but also for my own protection as well. He had been my life and lover for the last four years, so the possibility of me having come in contact with the disease was great. My body would not allow my brain to take in the information. All I could handle at that very moment was what was before me. While speaking, all I could do was shake my head. I could not register anything that Nico was saying to me. We spoke of things briefly for a moment before Nico and I shared a hug. Not an ordinary hug, though I could feel it would be our last as he said his goodbyes to me. I sobbed as his fragile arms wrapped around me. It was as though I could feel life slipping away from him. Surprisingly, I was not concerned with my own health. It was an indescribable feeling to me, one in which I would never wish on my worst enemy, not even Keisha. And just like that, I watched Nico walk away right out my life.

After he had left, I sat on the front steps to my house, going over all that had just taken place. The man that I loved whom I never thought could hurt me, had just told me that he had possibly given me a deadly disease that could take my life. I had so many mixed feelings about the entire thing. Was it all his fault? Had I pushed him too far? Was I only to think of myself and my health, or should I embrace him and be there for him in his last moments here on this earth? The questions were endless. I thought of my kids and what was to become of them in the event that I did have the disease and it did take my life. All the men I had been with, how was I ever going to tell them that they had been exposed to this infection as well? As bad as I knew that there was more at stake than just the obvious, I could not help returning to a place where the only person I could be concerned about was myself. It was selfish yet really a rational emotion. I guess it was just part of my grieving process. This was a big blow to me, and I had nowhere to go to feel a sense of relief. It is amazing how dangerous it could be becoming lost within your thoughts after learning unfortunate news. Sometimes your own thoughts can be more lethal than the bullet itself. When in this state things that would normally seem irrational otherwise begin to feel normal and an option making it easier to pull that trigger or slice your wrist or jump off that roof. All of which I had no plans on doing. My mind had already confirmed my prognosis for me, so there was no need for a doctor's diagnosis. My body had been telling me for months that something was wrong, but I was too determined not to listen. I started to see the dark circles. I was getting skinnier, and I wasn't wanting to eat anything. I was weak and I was beginning to see open lesions on my body. So now there was no reason to schedule the appointment that I had been meaning to schedule for days now to see the doctor about the persistent cough. I knew exactly what it was.

Chapter 17

Kesha (Wait, what?)

Gina, who was one of my proteges in training, had offered to drive me over to Candace's house and wait for me while I went in. I took her up on her offer and went. Walking up the long walkway to Candace's house felt a little weird since I had not been there in a while. This time, all I felt was emptiness. I had butterflies in my stomach and could feel the saliva in my mouth foaming up in efforts to lubricate my dry palette. I needed to shake this feeling off before knocking on Candace's door. I was unwilling to show her any signs of weakness. I gave myself a pep talk on how Candace was beneath me, and I was in control of my own destiny. So, if Nico was what I wanted, I would need to claim him as my own. Once that was over, it was time to confront Candace. Stopping short of the door, I closed my eyes and regained my composure one last time, placing my game face on.

Upon opening them, I saw Nico standing before me. I felt limp with joy, jumping into his arms, kissing him all over and holding him tightly. I knew I was not appearing to be that strong woman I normally appeared to be, but that did not matter since this was Nico, the only man I was willing to be vulnerable with. As I held him, I felt he was different, but I was unwilling to let anything tarnish this moment for me. Nico stood there motionless. His coldness made me change gears and take notice. He then looked at me and simply stated that this was not the time. I understood what he was saying, but I was in no mood to change my mind. Nico was very thin, and he seemed tired. He resembled one of those children in one of those 'Feed the Hungry' commercials, who had been suffering from malaria or starvation or something!

Rather than the vibrant man he normally appeared to be, he was withdrawn and quite pitiful looking if you ask me. I knew Candace must have done something to him to put him in such a state, which set me into a rage of anger. "What did she do to you, baby?" I began pacing back and forth outside of the house, searching for Candace, screaming her name, and slinging rocks at her window. I was determined to kill her for what she had done to Nico.

My rants and rave lasted for a few moments before Nico grabbed me and blurted out that he was HIV positive. "I have AIDS Keisha. It's in, it's end stages and I'm going to die. There's nothing else they can do for me."

I was not going to believe that because he was not gay, and he was a healthy man who had never been to jail. I chucked it up to another way that he was trying to protect Candace. "No, you don't, you liar." I was beyond mad at this point. I was furious. I could feel the blood vessels behind my eyes. Nico was going too far with this. I was unwilling to believe that he loved Candace that much to fabricate such a lie. It was a combination of disbelief, and the thought of someone else being taken away from me was just too much for me to bear. The last few months have been hard for me. My kids had been taken away from me. Tyrone was gone. All of my babies' fathers were locked up and I had no money and to add insult to injury, I was being evicted from my home of six years. My life was a complete disaster, and now Nico! The only thing I had left was trying to say he was leaving me too. I was not going to accept this news. I sat down on the curb in front of a house two doors down from Candace trying to regain some sense of composure.

Nico sat down next to me and looked at me, his hand too weak to squeeze mine so he just touched them. Now having my complete attention, Nico was looking me in the eyes touching my cheek as he said to me that I may be infected too, following by saying I needed to go and get tested. I did not think so. I had no symptoms of anything being wrong either way, positive or negative, he said. I needed to change my way of life. He was being serious, But I was in no mood for a lecture by him. I cut him off, saying that I was unwilling to listen to him getting angry by what he was saying to me. I did what I knew best, and that was to fight. I pushed and shoved him down, throwing punch after punch, kicking, and screaming, but there was no use and Nico was defenseless. He was not even able to block my punches. I stood up and I backed away from Nico's badly beaten body, lying in the grass, bleeding. I had just released all my anger and frustration on him for things that he did and for what he didn't do. I turned away and I left. But I knew the image of Nico that day would forever be embedded in my mind. I would never see Nico again alive after that day.

Chapter 18

Alexis (WHY ME?)

Nico died in the hospital alone. I had been trying to get to the hospital when the doctor called and told me he had passed. It seemed he had just been beaten up by someone and his body just could not recover. His funeral turned out to be an even bigger mess since Candace and Keisha found out what each other had done and fought over his grave site at the cemetery. It had turned out that Nico had two other children, all of whom mothers, had contracted the disease as well. Candace got tested and discovered she had gotten the disease too, but it winded up being too much for her to handle and she committed suicide in her house while her kids were sleeping. Her 16-year-old son found her lifeless body hanging in their basement one week after Nico's funeral.

As for Keisha, she left Baltimore and moved to Philadelphia, where I heard after losing everything and finding out she was HIV positive, she went crazy, knowing that she would infect as many men as she possibly could before she died. Police have been investigating her after over thirty men had come forth claiming to have been infected by her, according to the state health department. The last I had learned she was still living in Philly and was denying that she had even contracted the disease. As for me, I have been blessed, seeing to the fact that Nico and I had not used protection both times we were intimate. God has spared my life. I would like to believe that it was for me to do better for my children and show them what the face of survival really looks like. Even though the roads were hard, and some of the paths I had taken were all wrong I would like to think that it was all a lesson I could one day pass on to my loved ones on what not to do.

After Nico's death, I read the letter he had left for Nyla and myself. It stated that he had put over $100,000 in a trust account for Nyla. Also, he had listed me as his beneficiary to his $1,000,000 insurance policy. I could not believe Nico left all of this to us when he had other children out here. After investigating deeper, it was revealed that Nico had been unsure of the paternity of his other children. He was never in a relationship with any of the other women. Since, unlike me, they were aware of the gold mine he had been sitting on. So, I did what I thought was right. I did what any decent human being would do. I got all the children in question, tested for their paternity and I split the money equally between them. It turned out both children were indeed Nico's. Making sure to put their money safe and in a trust and keep in touch with them so that they could get to know their little sister, Nyla.

Once that was out of the way, Desmond and I became legal guardians to Candace's children. I felt it was the least I could do since I was unable to tell her of what I had done with Nico before she passed. I really did love that girl. She was my sister. Desmond had known about Nico and me all along. He said he had run into Nico at the hospital and Nico came clean. He said Nico had agreed to allow him to raise Nyla as his own. He explained to Desmond exactly what happened and why. He asked him never to reveal to Nyla the truth about her father's true identity, since it would only cause her more pain. He went on to say that I was a good person and that I had only been guilty of making a bad mistake. Desmond stated that Nico had admitted to him that he had fallen in love with me that night, and that he was grateful to God for allowing him the experience of true love, even if only for one night....

www.ingramcontent.com/pod-product-compliance
Lightning Source LLC
Chambersburg PA
CBHW050413030726
47503CB00006B/2165